That's Paris

An Anthology of Life, Love and Sarcasm in the City of Light

velvet morning
press

Published by Velvet Morning Press

ISBN-13: 978-0692340110
ISBN-10: 0692340114

Cover design by Vicki Lesage and Ellen Meyer

If you like *That's Paris* you might also like:

Editor's Note:

Four pieces in this anthology were originally written in French. You will find the French text, as it was submitted to us, following the English version of the story. We hope you enjoy this bilingual reading experience!

(ndlr : Quatre nouvelles de cette anthologie ont été écrites en français. Vous trouverez les textes originaux, comme ils nous ont été soumis, après nos traductions en anglais. Nous espérons que vous apprécierez cette expérience de lecture bilingue !)

To Paris, the always-inspiring City of Light

Table of Contents

Foreword

STEPHEN CLARKE

Paris has, in its literary career, produced countless millions of words. I myself have added more than a million to the count. Admittedly some of those were the same words over and over again. Note the repetition of "over" in that sentence, for example (and again in this one). But plenty have been more typically Parisian—classics like *"Métro"*, "Eiffel" and *"arrondissement"*, as well as slightly more esoteric terms along the lines of *"chambre de bonne"* (small attic room), *"carte de séjour"* (residence permit) and the highly versatile *"merde"* (surely you know what that means?)

The French have, of course, been especially adept at using their own words about Paris. In the fifteenth century, the poet François Villon praised Parisian women for their "good tongues" (a bit of medieval double entendre there); 200 years later Molière was poking fun at the city's snobs and hypocrites; Baudelaire did similar things in the 1800s (though under the depressing effect of absinthe); Balzac, Flaubert, Proust and Zola explored every *salon* and side-street in their novels; and by the end of the 1950s Raymond Queneau was satirizing all this French literary creativity in *Zazie dans le Métro*.

It's tempting to ask how much room is left for all us foreigners. And being a long-time Parisian resident, and therefore disproportionately fond of rhetorical questions, I will ask it: How much room is left for all us foreigners?

Well, fortunately, the answer is: *beaucoup*.

The list of non-French writers who have come to Paris and left their mark on literature may seem intimidating. To name just a few English-speakers, there have been Samuel Beckett, James Joyce, Gertrude Stein, Henry Miller and Ernest Hemingway. And we newcomers are meant to follow big names like that?

But no one should be discouraged from writing their own Parisian material just because a few famous people got here first. And after all, not all of the above wrote about Paris itself. Some of them came here just to enjoy the artistic freedom that the city offered, as well as (in some cases) the cheap booze and legal prostitution. And, most importantly, all of them were writing in their own style, ignoring everyone who'd come before them and (in some cases) ignoring rules of grammar and even meaning, too. If Joyce can get away with passages like this one from *Ulysses*, we mere mortals can get away with anything: "His lips lipped and mouthed fleshless lips of air: mouth to her moomb. Oomb, allwombing tomb." Those two sentences were first published in Paris, so there's hope for everyone.

These days, most writers seem to have got that brand of modernism out of their systems (though I admit I once wrote a story in nonsense language, using an invented alphabet that was impossible to print—I wonder why that never got published?), and have decided to focus on ideas. You might think that such a small, concentrated city—about ten times smaller than London in surface area—would eventually dry up as a source of ideas, but luckily, unlike the red tuna served up in all the sushi restaurants here, Parisian ideas seem to be an eternally sustainable resource.

This, I think, has nothing to do with the city's reputation as an intellectual, philosophical capital. Too much intellectualizing can stifle ideas rather than encouraging them to flow. It seems to me that the best Parisian writing, in English anyway, is more down-to-earth than that—it's a direct result of the head-on culture shock that most of us experience when we arrive here. It's not just that the language is different, it's that Paris does everything its own way, which is generally the exact opposite of the way we do everything back home.

This contrariness is not Paris's fault, of course. Parisians can live how they like in their city, and it's up to us to cope (or give up and run away, as some people do). It is the sheer confrontation that sparks so much writing.

The shock of the new pervades every aspect of life. I wrote an entire book, *A Year in the Merde*, sparked by two tiny details of my new Parisian existence: First, the people in the building next to mine seemed to think that it was OK to let their dogs use the pavement outside my front door as a public toilet, presumably on the grounds that they personally were in little danger of treading in it; and secondly, the first (and last) time I ordered tea in a Parisian café, the waiter brought me a pot of warmish water, an empty cup and a tea bag still in its wrapper. There was no milk, and I had to make the tea myself, so basically I was paying a small fortune for their dishwashing.

I expanded these two traumas into a novel about an Englishman who moves to Paris, gets his shoes dirty and tries to open a café that will make decent tea. (I should stress to everyone who hasn't read it that I did add in a couple more ideas to fill things out a little.)

Everyone who comes to live in Paris has their own

merde/teabag experience, be it with partners, colleagues, neighbours, bureaucrats, service providers, drivers, language, food, drink, or public transport—in short, with everything and everybody.

Because Parisians are trapped inside their *périphérique* ring road, extraordinary experiences somehow become more concentrated, and more diverse. There are twenty *arrondissements*, but each of those is divided up into tiny *quartiers* with their own personality. In my book *Paris Revealed* I even tried to describe the distinct groups of people who take the different *Métro* lines at various points along their routes.

Ah yes, the *Métro*, where I seem to spend half my life. At rush hours, getting on and off trains can be a martial art, or at the very least a feat of international diplomacy. It's not that Parisians are aggressive—they just have very little space in which to do their Parisian things, and they expect you to understand the system instantly.

For example, there is a *Métro* junction at Stalingrad station, on Line 7. On the southbound platform, two narrow staircases lead passengers down into the tunnels that take them to Lines 2 and 5. As soon as a train stops at this platform, the carriages nearest the stairs empty like a pressure cooker. Everyone dashes for those two openings, creating an instant logjam that is only released when the people at the front get up speed in the stairway, and rocket down. If you are an innocent tourist, trying to read your *Métro* map, wondering how to get to Line 2 or 5, or checking that your bag/phone/wallet/partner/kids are where you want them, you will be treated to an onslaught of Parisian elbows, insults and groans of frustration. You have blocked the urgent flow of Parisian life through its cruelly restricted arteries, albeit for only two or three seconds, and you're being punished for it.

The same scenario happens at every *Métro* junction, at every pedestrian crossing, wherever Parisians interact.

Each aspect of Parisian life has its rules—which café table to sit at if you're only having a drink or if there are only two of you; what time on a Friday afternoon you can actually expect people to attend a meeting; where a taxi driver might agree to take you, or not; whom to call *tu* and *vous*; whom to kiss and how many times—the list is endless, and some of the rules are totally different to towns just an hour away.

People are forced to encounter Paris close-up and face-to-face, and the city has so many moods that almost no one will have exactly the same experience. This book contains more than 30 encounters, by almost as many writers, each one with their own story to tell.

The title of the book has a story behind it, too—"Ca, c'est Paris" is the name of a song made famous in the 1920s by Mistinguett, a hugely popular music-hall singer with an accent as Parisian as the Eiffel Tower, who sang that Paris "has perfected the art of giving herself." The writers in this book have all, in their own way, accepted the city's generous offer, and are now sharing their personal Paris with you, dear reader. I for one would like to say "*merci beaucoup.*"

Stephen Clarke, Paris.

Stephen's latest book about Paris is *Dirty Bertie: an English King Made in France*, the true story of King Edward VII's outrageous exploits in nineteenth-century Paris at the time when the boulevards, the can-can, Montmartre and Impressionism were all in their infancy. He saw it all happen and was even the first guest—French or otherwise—to climb the Eiffel Tower.

Gizzards, Wine and Daily Bread

The French Table, a Test of Mettle

AUDREY M. CHAPUIS

The French table presents many challenges to the average American. The first is one of stamina. I will never forget my inaugural 12-hour meal in Paris. Well, to be exact, it was two meals, but one ran right into the other. Lunch began at noon, and the conversation carried us through dinner until midnight. At one point, I broke the spell and went for a quick walk—my poor glutes couldn't take any more sitting in my wrought iron chair—but I was the only one.

Apart from such marathon feasts, your derrière better be ready to sit for a good three hours even for an ordinary weekend dinner.

The second test is one of table manners. I've learned not to be ashamed when the children at the table brandish their steak knives with more grace and agility than me. Or when my dinner companion asks why I switch my utensils from hand to hand to manage a piece of meat. Or when someone points out that, technically, it's rude to cut salad. (Why am I the only one with salad dressing on my chin when shoveling a lettuce leaf the size of a quilt into my mouth?)

But the third, and most important, is the challenge of the food itself.

We simply haven't been introduced to many of the foods that commonly feature on French menus. Of course, this is changing as the foodie culture gains popularity in the United States. These days, you can find restaurants dedicated to using all parts of the pig and hear tales of Manhattan investment bankers retiring at age 30 to become artisanal cheese makers in Vermont. But still, in many cases, French food has the power to shock Americans. Or, if not shock us, at least leave us and our taste buds shivering in trepidation.

The French get a huge kick out of this. They like putting your francophilia to the test. "Oh, you like our wine and our literature, but what do you think about our head cheese?"

The quest for full French acceptance consists of five levels:

Level One: Things Found in the Forest or Pond
Level Two: Mold
Level Three: Parts Cruelly Prepared
Level Four: Viscera
Level Five (The Ultimate Test): The Animal's Periphery, a.k.a. Face and Feet

In general, French people love to discuss food. When they dine with an American, it's a chance for them to reminisce about their favorite dishes while simultaneously freaking out their guest.

Host: "Have you tried frog legs? How about *escargot*?" (Level One)
Guest: "Sure! It's easy to love anything bathed in garlic, butter and herbs."
Host: "I'm glad to hear you're not like most Americans.

Here, try this nice *Pont-L'Evêque*." (Level Two) You're presented with the source of the stench that's been knocking you over for the past three hours, the king of stinky cheese, which has been ripening at room temperature on the counter.

Guest: "Why thank you, that's delicious." They're annoyed when you don't protest.

Host: "And *foie gras*? We've heard some American cities have banned this delicacy!" (Level Three)

Guest: "Actually, I think the ban's been lifted." Now, they're truly disappointed.

Host: "What about blood sausage? *Andouillette*? Tripe? Kidneys?" At this point, they're trying anything to stump you, but when you've finally passed Level Four, you may be the proud recipient of a French nod-frown of "not bad."

But, I'm ashamed to admit, I flunked Level Five.

For years, a friend originally from Lyon, which some French people consider to be the culinary capital of the country, had heard me repeatedly profess my love for various scary French foods and seen me flaunt my hearty appetite. So she decided to test my mettle once and for all.

One evening, she invited me for a simple, light dinner outside on one of those mild summer nights in Paris when twilight hits late and lasts long.

As the *apéritif* began, I should have recognized the bad omen lurking in the lawn. A black cat hovered over a patch in the grass, unmoving for what seemed like an hour. Finally, he pounced in a frenzied, brief attack. In the alien blue evening light, it was difficult to see what he had succeeded in capturing, so the guests strolled over, champagne flutes in hand, to discover the cat batting around the detached head of a gopher. Fascinated, we watched the grisly game.

At the same time, our hostess laid out the repast: fresh bread, a bottle of cellar-cooled red, and two large salads, one of *museau*, the other of *pied de cochon*, which in French sound beautiful, but when translated are immediately stripped of their appeal: snout salad and pig foot salad.

In concept, I didn't object. Our hostess is an amazing cook, and I knew she was serving the best. Indeed, the other diners dug in and sang the salads' delicious praises.

The first forkful of cartilage did me in. Usually I have no problem with texture. Chewy, slimy, gooey, mushy? No problem. But I had the distinct impression that I was affectionately nibbling on a cold pig's ear. It was too much. Of course, I kept my proud mouth shut and hoped my uneaten salads were somewhat hidden in the shadows.

Did I imagine a mischievous crinkle at the corner of my friend's mouth when she offered me seconds? Perhaps we both knew I had been vanquished, that I hadn't passed Level Five.

The guests at the table elegantly chewed their thin pink squares of *museau* and *pied*. The cat was still busy with his savage playtime in the lawn. Only I seemed to be on the sidelines. I tore off a chunk of baguette, took a big swig of Burgundy and promised myself to do better the next time I'm presented with a gourmet foot on my plate.

Signs, Signs, Everywhere Signs
VICKI LESAGE

I didn't mean to complain. I was grateful for the heaps of wedding presents I received before The Big Day even arrived. I'd be marrying *Monsieur* Perfect in one month's time, and my American friends and family would descend on Paris *en masse* for the occasion. I wanted to wrap up as many odds and ends as possible before they overtook the city—and my normally *très* organized life—for one week.

Number one on my list: writing eleventy thank you notes. Never mind my chicken-scrawl penmanship or the fact I hadn't handwritten anything other than our exorbitant rent check recently. The primary pain in my derrière was getting my out-of-practice hands on some damn thank you cards.

It was August, and except for the occasional tumbleweed and busload of tourists, the residential streets of Paris were deserted as Parisians took their annual month-long vacation. The neighborhood *papeteries* had closed their ancient doors, leaving me no choice but to trek to Auchan, the French megastore that's just like Target, except it's full of *la merde* and you usually leave empty-handed and broken-hearted. So, actually, nothing like Target.

Entering the behemoth, I pushed through a turnstile and passed an imposing security guard. Dude, please. I wouldn't dream of stealing a tube of toothpaste or a pair of socks. But that's only because I couldn't locate them in this maze of a store.

With no directory or overhead signs to guide me, I braved the store with trepidation, working my way around in a counter-clockwise direction. My stomach growled. I picked up the pace, hoping to make it out before full-on hunger hit. After the Earth orbited the sun a few times, I found the stationery aisle, next to shoddy children's clothing and cheap champagne. But of course.

The paper goods selection was pathetic. I'd seen fancier displays in dumpsters. Pack of sequined stationery? Check. Cards sold one-by-one, for the low price of 5.99 euros? Check. Kids' birthday invitations with scary mimes? Check. Birthday cards yellowed around the edges? Check.

But no thank you cards. Not even a pack of plain white cards. My tummy roared. How long had I been wandering this fluorescent hellscape? At that point, I would have settled for two sticks to rub together and send smoke-signal greetings—but they didn't have those either. Not to be picky, but I couldn't very well send a "Sorry for your loss" card to my grandma. Though considering the generosity of her gift, I suppose it *had* been a significant loss to her bank account.

Should I cave in and buy the ugly cards? Splurge on the expensive ones and skip dinner for a month? Or worse—skip WINE for a month? As I hesitated, my cell phone rang.

"Hi sweetie," I said, answering the call from my fiancé. "The phone is gonna cut out any second. I'm stuck in the purgatory of Auchan."

"*Oh là là.* Get out while you still can!"

I hung up the phone, promising to call once I was free. I abandoned my shopping expedition. I refused to show my appreciation by sending a card a clown had vomited on. And I was growing grouchier by the minute. I needed calories and fresh air, *tout de suite*.

I headed to the checkouts and squeezed past a lady unloading her cart. Just as the exit was within reach, like hopeful rays of light shining down from the heavens and angels singing "Hallelujah," a cashier wearing way too much make-up stopped me in my tracks.

"*Mademoiselle*, you can't exit that way. You must go around." I suspected she was frowning, but her uneven lipstick made it hard to tell.

I looked up at the sign that said "Exit" and turned back to her, confused. "But, *Madame*, this is the exit, no?"

"You. Must. Go. Around."

I wanted to say, "Oh yeah? And who's gonna make me?" But the burly security guard materialized and blocked my path.

"Is there a problem?" he asked, clearly hoping there would be a problem and he'd get to see a little action.

"I'm not stealing," I said as my face reddened. Everyone in the checkout line stared at me. "I just couldn't find what I was looking for." Except my French wasn't quite that smooth so it was more like, "I don't steal. I don't find the thing I search." This didn't win me any points.

"*Mademoiselle*." Now the cashier was mad, as if *I* had been wasting *her* time. "Like I said, you must go around." She pointed to the entrance. Which was the same as the exit, but required going all the way around the checkouts, down the front aisle of the store, and back through one of the turnstiles. Just to end up two millimeters from where I was currently standing.

I considered making a break for it, but Officer I-Don't-Think-So-Honey read my mind and stepped in front of me.

"Fine!" I let out an exasperated sigh, then squeezed back past the stupid lady with the stupid cart. I walked all the stupid way around their stupid store, shaking my head and muttering under my breath like the lunatic I'd become.

As I neared the entrance and was about to pass through the turnstile, the same blasted security guard stopped me. What now? What could I have possibly done wrong? Was I supposed to push the turnstile with my left hand? Tap dance as I shimmied through? Whisper the secret password in Officer I-Don't-Think-So-Honey's ear?

"*Mademoiselle*, you're using the wrong exit."

"*C'est pas possible!*" I threw my hands in the air. "You've got to be kidding me. The cashier told me to go this way. You were there, remember? It was two seconds ago. Will I ever get out of this hellhole?"

I said that last part in English, and the security guard raised an eyebrow in confusion. He then pointed to a sign over one of the turnstiles: *Sortie Sans Achat*. Exit Without Purchase.

This infernal store, a store with literally millions of products, was so accustomed to people leaving without purchasing any of its crap that there was even a sign for it. Perhaps time would be better spent, oh, I don't know, stocking products people actually want to buy?

The store's weekly management meetings must go something like this:

Assistant Manager: "OK, next on the list, the stationery department. What types of new cards could we add to the collection? If we offer a wide variety, we could boost sales."

Manager: "What? No. That's way too much work."

Assistant Manager: "But…"

Manager: "Plus, if we offer a limited selection, they'll be forced to buy from the stock we already have, and we'll finally get rid of those horrible cards from '86. What was Gérard thinking? We'll never sell those birthday ones with squirrels in sequined dresses."

Assistant Manager: "They're pretty funny, though."

Manager: "True. There's nothing funnier than an animal in a dress. Oh, by the way, can you hang this new Exit Without Purchase sign? It just came in from You Shouldn't Need a Sign For That R Us."

Assistant Manager: "*Très classe!* Could use a few sequins, though."

While Auchan must not get much business, You Shouldn't Need a Sign For That R Us clearly does. I see absurd signs all over Paris.

When boutiques redo their window displays, they post a sign to the effect of "Window Display in Progress." You don't say. Here I thought this store sold naked mannequins.

Though I wonder: Do they hang a sign in the naked mannequin store so people know the window dressing is finished? "This window display is NOT in progress. Buy your naked mannequins today!" Without a sign, people would stand in front of the window for days, waiting to see the final arrangement.

Or how about at McDonald's? Not that I've ever been there, cough, cough. You'll stop by the Golden Arches, in the mood for a Royale with Cheese. But, *zut alors!* The picture of the juicy burger on the menu is covered with a sign stating: *Indisponible: Victime de Son Succès.* Sold Out: Victim of Its Success.

The Royale with Cheese is so popular it's sold out! Congrats! But wait... the Royale with Cheese and Bacon is still available. How is that possible? Is the bacon stapled to the cheese? How come I can't get the burger without the bacon? And, more importantly, why did they waste time making a sign instead of getting more Royales with Cheese?

I spotted the best sign on the day I nearly electrocuted myself. I was strolling this fair city with my fiancé, one hand clasped in his, the other swinging freely by my side, when I nearly made contact with a live wire dangling from a building. How did I know it was a live wire? Because a vinyl sign affixed to it informed: *Haute Tension: Danger de Mort.* High Voltage: Danger of Death.

At first glance, it seemed thoughtful of them to have put up a warning sign. Thanks, guys! I'll refrain from touching the cable, tempting as it is. But upon further reflection, I had a few questions. How many people zapped themselves with the cable while the workers were out purchasing the sign? Unless they had an interim sign that said, "Don't touch the wire—we're out buying a better sign."

And, I can't believe I have to ask this yet again, but why buy a sign instead of solving the problem? "This here wire? Oh yeah, it'll kill you. That's why we don't want to risk fixing it. Like our sign, though? It's so vinyl-y!"

I survived that incident, and I survived Auchan. Barely. I'd escaped the clutches of that blasted store without eating anyone's arm.

As I returned from my fruitless shopping trip, I fumed. The employees had been so concerned about me following the correct process to exit their labyrinthine store that no one even bothered to ask why I hadn't purchased anything. No offer to help me find what I was looking for, no apology for having wasted my time. What happened to *service clientèle*?

I called my fiancé and vented. He sympathized with me. He was usually proud of his native country but could admit its flaws. Reason #248 why I loved him.

"If it's not too much trouble, do you mind picking up a baguette on the way home?" he asked.

With *plaisir*. I was famished.

I swung by our local *boulangerie*, but was greeted with closed doors. Oh, right. August. Like the rest of the neighborhood, they had closed up shop for vacation.

Before I turned green and Hulk-ed out, I noticed a sign. A pretty little sign with the perfectly neat handwriting that all French people seem to have mastered. "We are closed for the summer holidays, but invite you to visit one of the following *boulangeries* for your bread needs. Thank you and good day." And they listed the three nearest bakeries.

My rage subsided, and I remembered why I loved this gloriously infuriating city. It may hide its thank you cards and Royales with Cheese. It might electrocute you. But when it counts, Parisians are there for you.

They will never send you home without your bread.

La Vie de Vin

DryChick

I've always had romantic notions of Paris, just like any other francophile. I learned the language well enough to get by on my own, and had good friends who lived there. So when I visited, I considered myself almost Parisian.

I also loved wine and drank plenty of it when I was there.

I had a favorite sidewalk café, Café Pierre on place de la République, where I always ordered rosé and a *salade de chèvre chaud*. My usual waiter with the ponytail always treated me kindly and with respect, suppressing any sign of a grimace when I first pronounced *chaud* with a hard "d." Without embarrassing me, he repeated my order slowly and clearly so I could note the proper pronunciation, for which I was grateful. And later he complimented me—in French—for trying so hard to speak the language. French waiters don't have a reputation for being nice to customers, especially foreigners (think the Griswolds in *National Lampoon's European Vacation*), but he seemed genuine. Or maybe he hoped for a fat tip from the foreigner (which I happily obliged).

So Paris was the last place I wanted to visit after I quit drinking and became "dry."

Yes, I was worried I would be tempted to indulge in wine. But I had an even deeper, more overriding fear: Maybe I wouldn't love Paris as much as I used to. The thought was heartbreaking.

I loved Paris so much that I never wanted to live there, even though I've had the opportunity to do so. I wanted it to be the special place I fled to when I needed the three Cs: culture, color and cuisine, which truly nourished my soul. (And champagne, of course.)

I longed to join the young, hip Parisians who brought bottles of wine to the banks of the Canal Saint-Martin every evening. They laughed and imbibed as the sun set, the epitome of *joie de vivre*.

Nearby was Chez Prune, another café I used to frequent. Last time, I went alone on my birthday. I ordered a carafe of house red and a cheese plate, and sat facing the canal, surrounded by those young, hip Parisians who had moved on from the canal to drink and smoke at wobbly sidewalk tables.

The waitress was foreign herself and took pity on my French. I was feeling really good, until my food and wine were delivered.

The snotty French girl smoking a cigarette at the next table burst out laughing and said to her friends, "*La touriste* needs a big spoon to eat her food."

"Is she going to drink and eat all of that herself?" her equally snooty friend added.

My face fell. I looked down at the plate and acknowledged that it was definitely big enough for two, but I hadn't known that when I'd ordered. And the carafe—well, I was pleased with it (and that was just for starters!)

I gave them a death stare that said, "I understood all

of that, and I won't dignify it with a response." In reality, I didn't know how to respond.

Defiantly, I ate my cheese and bread, drank my wine and promptly ordered another carafe. The bitchy birds finally left, and I started to cry. The waitress asked me what was wrong, and I told her in broken, sobbing *français* what the nasty French girls had said.

"Et c'est mon anniversaire!" I added for effect. She grabbed my hand and brought me to the bar. She told the bartender that this poor girl needed a birthday shot, and that she would join me in having one.

In a better mood now, I skipped out of Chez Prune and moved on to another little restaurant. I sat down in a zebra print chair in the corner, surrounded by stacks of magazines with French versions of *Hello* and *OK*. I ordered more wine and immersed myself in celebrity gossip. Suddenly, I heard a table in the back singing "Happy Birthday" in English. I felt as if they were singing to me. The waitress apologized for the noise, and I told her I didn't mind: It was my birthday too! She left and reappeared with a slice of cake.

My faith in Paris had been restored.

So returning sober was going to be bittersweet. There would be no drinking rosé at Café Pierre or the house red at Chez Prune. Could I even enjoy cheese or *steak-frites* without wine?

Yes. Paris has much more to offer, and I couldn't avoid the situation forever. I planned a weekend back to my beloved city and packed a bottle of my favorite alcohol-free red wine in case I had any cravings.

My friends who lived in the 10th *arrondissement* made sure I had amazing meals with fancy lemonades, polished off with mind-blowing desserts, which I savored bite by bite. Instead of my usual visits to the *caves à vin*, we hit the Marais for teas from Mariage Frères and Palais des Thés, where I discovered teas could be as varied—and as expensive—as wine.

But the canal still beckoned.

So I borrowed a wine glass from my friends and headed there with my alcohol-free bottle of red.

The sun was setting on a beautiful fall day, and I brushed away leaves to sit amongst the crowd. I poured myself a glass and smiled. A boat navigated its way past the Antoine et Lili boutique and under the hallmark blue cage-wire bridge.

I was relieved. Nothing had changed. The young, hip Parisians were too busy laughing, drinking and smoking to notice my wine was alcohol-free. I felt silly that I had made such a big deal about it. The problem—as always—was solely with me.

As I walked back to my hotel, I passed more of my old favorite haunts. The sidewalk outside La Patache was swollen with trendy Parisians smoking cigarettes and drinking wine. The last time I was there, I was outshone by an older woman who seemed perfectly fine until she abruptly stood up and started Greek dancing to what I can only imagine was the *My Big Fat Greek Wedding* soundtrack in her head. She stomped around the bar for a good half hour, all the while watching herself in the mirror. At first, people laughed and clapped, but after 10 minutes, they went back to their *charcuterie* and didn't take further notice. However, I remained fascinated by her because I had never seen anyone visibly drunk in Paris before.

Ironically, the weekend I returned to Paris dry, the newspapers were talking about a growing problem with "Le Binge Drinking." (Of course they used the English version of the word because the French never translate anything negative, as if it were a plague sent from outside their shores, and they're not to blame for it.)

Maybe I was finally ahead of Paris on something.

On my walk home, I spotted a few new bars where I

easily pictured myself, chatting up the bartenders in my
"charming" (i.e. crap) French. I could've gone in, but
immediately thought, "What would I order?" I could be
chic and order an espresso, but then I'd be up all night.

And I was already dreaming about my *pain au chocolat*
and dentist's rinse cup of cappuccino the next morning
before I headed back to London. (Paris, I will never
understand why your *boulangeries* serve the most decadent
pâtisseries but have utter disdain for caffeinated beverages
to go with it.) No, better to head home, *sans* alcohol, but
full of new memories of my favorite city.

I'm probably the only person who has ever brought
alcohol-free wine to Paris. And upon reflection, I'm so
glad to realize I could have actually done without it.

This One Time in Paris

SARAH DEL RIO

So I thought I'd start this off with a multiple-choice quiz. (Don't stress. It's only one question.)

Who is the best choice to write an essay for a book about Paris?

Choose one of the following options:

A) Someone who lives in Paris
B) Someone who has traveled extensively in Paris
C) Someone who has visited Paris even just the one time
D) Someone who has at the very least read a book about Paris
E) Any/all of the above people will do, as long as it isn't someone who has never been to Paris and knows absolutely nothing about it.

I don't think I need to tell you the answer is E. Pretty obvious, right?

Yet here I am.

That's right. Not only have I never been to Paris, I've never been to France at all. Nope. Not even once. Sure, I've been to other places in Europe—in fact, I even married a European. Just not a European from France (or "France-man," as some call them.)

I've never even read anything about Paris. Not a single thing. If hard-pressed, I think I could *maybe* come up with three facts[1] about Paris:

1. Something something Marcel Marceau.
2. The Phantom of the Opera lives there and runs around yelling "THE PHANTOM OF THE OPERAAAAAAA" in everyone's face all the time.
3. There's some sort of famous tower in Paris. Did you guys know about this? I have to say, it's not exactly an original design. I've seen a lot of knick-knacks on clearance at HomeGoods that look AWFULLY SIMILAR.

Still, despite my appalling lack of Parisian knowledge and experience, I do have a short tale to tell about *La Ville-Lumière*. (Yes, I did just look that up on Wikipedia. Wanna fight about it?) While I myself have never been to Paris, I just happen to know someone who has.

It was 1999, and my friend Tommy was a young gay man full of hopes, dreams, four years of high school French and a yearning desire to visit the grave of Edith Piaf. Fortunately for him, one of his good friends relocated from the United States to Vichy, and a once-impossible dream of visiting France suddenly became a Much More Affordable Opportunity.

Almost as soon as his travel plans were set in motion, I was summoned to Tommy's apartment and assigned the tedious job of helping him fill his suitcase with what I'll generously call "*le Costume d'Eurotrash*." Tommy also asked me to help him brush up on his French, which was rusty since he hadn't spoken a word of it since high

---

[1] Not actual facts.

school. In retrospect, this may have been a stupid idea, since my own French is limited to the following expressions:

* *Bonjour*
* *Bon voyage*
* *Merci beaucoup*
* *Hors d'œuvres*
* *Au Bon Pain*

Oh well. I did the best I could.

Anyway. The time came for Tommy to wing his way to France. He spent a few marvelous weeks in Vichy with a group of warm, welcoming young people who taught him as much about the culture and language as he wanted to know. Within a very short period of time, and thanks to a wealth of patience and encouragement from his new French *amis*, he became more competent in the French language than he had ever been.

By the end of his stay in Vichy, Tommy was speaking French around the clock. He might not have been fluent, exactly, but he was MAKING AN EFFORT. Which is more than can be said for most American tourists.

Sadly, all good things must come to an end, and Tommy's stay in the cordial French countryside did as well. He packed his bags and caught a train to Paris, where he was scheduled to fly back to the United States the next day.

Upon his arrival in Paris, Tommy had some time to kill, so he found a café in which to drink a few glasses of wine and enjoy his last delicious meal in France. With his newfound cultural confidence, he lifted his hand to attract a nearby waiter's attention.

"*Excusez-moi*," he politely said to the waiter. "*Un vin blanc, s'il vous plaît.*"

The waiter looked down his nose at Tommy and

replied in cold, perfect English:

"Don't even try."

And that's everything I know about Paris.

View From a Bridge

Half Past Midnight
DIDIER QUÉMENER

Louis-Philippe Bridge, île Saint-Louis, half past midnight.

"If I were you, I wouldn't opt for a late night dip. The Seine is a bit chilly this time of year…"

Mélusine didn't turn around.

"You can think whatever you'd like, but you're not me," she said under her breath. "So you can't judge a situation you know nothing about."

Cigarette in hand, Damien stared at the water, illuminated only by lights from the evening's last fly boats.

"In any case, you won't get very far. With all of the people around here to call for help, they'll drag you out in less than ten minutes. Your plan is far from perfect!"

He approached the railing and leaned against it.

"And I'll be frank with you: I'd be kind of annoyed about wasting my cigarette after lighting up only a minute ago." He took a drag.

"Who asked you to? I didn't. Go along your merry way and do your little display somewhere else."

"I see," he said. "You're a tough character. But at the

moment, I'm not the one putting on a show. You are."

Damien turned to face her.

"I'm Damien. And you?"

"What difference does it make?" she asked sharply.

"Well, if I know your name, I'll come here, right to this spot, to see you at every half past midnight. Just to make sure you're OK."

"I already have a psychiatrist. I don't need a second. And it's Mélusine." For the first time, she looked at Damien.

"Your psychiatrist's name is Mélusine? That's unusual!"

"You're a little slow, aren't you?" she said, shaking her head. "That's my name: Mélusine."

"Well, it is unusual."

"Do you ever come down to earth and stop talking in circles?" she asked in annoyance.

"Rarely. I'm not convinced that most of the human race is truly worth that effort. But from time to time, through a chance encounter, one can discover something charming…"

"Uh-oh. The outdated pick-up line that goes all the way back to the disco era! Did it ever work, even back then? I don't think so."

Silence. Once again, Damien looked at the lights flickering in the calm water. Mélusine, filled with anger and frustration, studied him.

"Why am I even wasting my time?" she asked. "First of all, I was here before you, so at least be polite and leave me alone. And keep your philosophy lessons for your next chance encounter!"

"Let me guess," he said. "This is all very recent. It happened perhaps two or three weeks ago. You thought he was the love of your life. He was attractive. Even his little flaws didn't bother you. They made you smile. Then, one evening, he came home late. The reason? A few extra drinks with his friends. It happened a second time, then a third…"

Mélusine listened, her mouth half open.

"One day, without asking yourself why, you started doubting. That's perfectly normal. It's human instinct, you know. An evening that he came home late, while he was in the shower, you had a look at his cell phone. You didn't know what you wanted to find, but you persisted. And then you quickly understood those so-called evenings with his buddies actually had a Spanish accent, was about five feet eight and had long, brown hair. Those 'evenings' were called Melinda."

Damien took a final drag on his cigarette. Spellbound, Mélusine only had the strength to take one step toward him. Finally, after several long minutes, her rage poured forth.

"You bastard!" she shouted, approaching the edge of the bridge. "You bastard! You're one of his goddamn friends, aren't you? He sent you because she dumped him and now he regrets his bullshit? Poor idiots. That's what both of you are: two poor idiots!"

Damien smashed his cigarette butt into the ground. He didn't flinch.

"How do you know the whole story?" Mélusine asked. "He told you everything? All the gory details… No? Well, I'll tell you the details. You'll see. I'll paint the real picture. I'll tell you all about him and that girl—that bitch!"

Hot tears ran down her cheeks, reddened from the cold air.

"I'm really a fool," she said, the anger in her voice turning to pain.

"I'm not one of his friends. Not even an acquaintance. I'm here for you—not for him. And as I told you, I'll come to see you at this same place over and over at half past midnight if that's what it takes! Until I'm sure all of this is behind you. When this becomes a distant memory in the depths of your heart, when you forget the details, when you move forward."

Mélusine looked Damien straight in the eye.

"Who are you, then? How do you know all of this? Tell me." Her voice was calm.

Damien glanced up at the starry night. Mechanically and without knowing why, Mélusine did the same. The full moon lit their faces.

"Do you remember your twin?"

That question was the last one Mélusine felt like hearing. Her legs trembled like those of a newborn.

"Do you remember?" he repeated.

"Of course I remember… No, what I mean is I don't remember, but I know the whole story."

"Ask your mother for his real first name. Not the one they gave him for the records, but the name your parents wanted to give him if…"

"You're crazy! Call my mother at this hour? She'd have a stroke!"

"Do it."

Not really knowing what she should do, Mélusine groped around in her bag until she found her phone. She scrolled down to her mother's number and dialed before she could change her mind.

"Mom? It's me. Yes, everything's fine. Don't worry."

"What's going on?" Her mother's groggy voice crackled across the line. "Do you know what time it is?"

"Yes, I know… Listen, I have an important question. What was Arthur's real first name?"

"What? What are you talking about?"

"Arthur, my twin. What was his name? I mean, what did you want to call him if…"

Mélusine lowered her head and covered her other ear to better hear her mother's words.

"I can't hear… Speak louder!"

"Mel, what has gotten into you? Asking such questions in the middle of the night!"

"I have to know, dammit! I'm not asking for the world! What difference does it make after all of these years?"

"Before your birth, your father and I decided on names. You were born first, and we gave you the name Mélusine. Your brother arrived a few moments later... lifeless."

"I know all of that! But my question?"

"Considering the circumstances, we were too distraught to give him the name we'd planned... But we had to give him a name for official records. Randomly, we chose 'Arthur.' We were in complete emotional turmoil. We were happy because you were healthy, yet devastated as we held your brother. His name would have been Damien."

Mélusine's telephone tumbled to the bridge. She looked up, searching for Damien. The sidewalk was empty. She turned around, but she was alone. On the ground, the smoke from his cigarette dissipated little by little. In her heart, his words echoed like a soothing melody:

I'll come here, right to this spot, to see you at every half past midnight.

Minuit et demi

DIDIER QUÉMENER

Pont Louis-Philippe, île Saint-Louis : minuit et demi.

— A votre place, j'éviterais le grand saut du bain de minuit. La Seine est un peu fraîche à cette époque de l'année.

Mélusine ne se retourna pas.

— Libre à vous de penser comme bon vous semble mais le fait est que vous n'êtes pas moi et que, par conséquent, vous ne pouvez pas juger une situation qui vous échappe, bafouilla-t-elle.

Cigarette à la main, Damien fixait les reflets lumineux sur le fleuve que les derniers bateaux-mouches éclairaient.

— De toute façon, vous n'irez pas bien loin. Ils vous sortiront de là en moins de dix minutes avec tout ce monde autour pour alerter les secours. Votre histoire est plutôt mal engagée !

Il s'approcha du parapet et s'accouda.

— En fait, je vais vous dire franchement : ça m'ennuierait quand même un peu de la gaspiller alors que je viens juste de l'allumer, dit-il agitant les cendres de sa cigarette par-dessus son épaule gauche.

— Ne vous sentez surtout pas obligé ! Je ne vous ai rien demandé. Passez votre chemin et allez faire votre numéro ailleurs.

— Je vois. Une coriace. Sauf que pour le moment, vous êtes celle qui se donne en spectacle, pas moi, ironisa-t-il.

Damien fit un quart de tour dans sa direction.

— Moi c'est Damien. Et vous ?

— Ça changera quoi ? rétorqua-t-elle sèchement.

— Ça changera que je reviendrai ici vous voir, au même endroit, chaque lendemain à minuit et demi précis... Histoire de faire le point.

— J'ai déjà un psy. Mélusine. Pas besoin d'un deuxième, ajouta-t-elle s'adressant à Damien en le regardant pour la première fois.

— Votre psy s'appelle Mélusine ? C'est pas banal !

— Un peu lent à ce que je vois, dit-elle secouant la tête de gauche à droite, c'est mon prénom : Mélusine.

— Ah oui, c'est bien ce que je disais : pas banal.

— Dites, ça vous arrive de redescendre sur terre et de cesser de vous écouter parler de temps en temps ? lança-t-elle visiblement agacée.

— Rarement, répliqua-t-il instantanément, je ne suis pas convaincu que la majorité de la race humaine en vaille vraiment la peine. Mais parfois en faisant de nouvelles rencontres fortuites, on se raccroche à quelque chose de presque charmant et vivant.

— Oh-oh... La bonne vieille technique de drague lourde et ringarde qui date de la fin de l'ère disco ! Tellement faux, ça sonne tellement creux et faux !

Un court silence s'était installé. Damien regardait de nouveau les dernières lumières sur l'eau qui retrouvait son calme nocturne. Mélusine le dévisageait, colérique et crispée.

— Mais qu'est-ce que je fous à perdre mon temps ? s'exclama-t-elle. D'abord, j'étais là avant vous.

Alors ayez la politesse de me laisser en paix. Et gardez vos leçons de philosophie pour vos prochaines rencontres comme vous dites !

— Laissez-moi deviner… C'est tout récent, deux ou trois semaines, tout au plus. Vous voyiez en lui l'homme de votre vie. Il était beau, vous aimiez même ses petits défauts. Ses petites manies vous donnaient le sourire. Puis un soir il est rentré un peu tard. Le prétexte ? Une soirée un peu longue avec ses potes. Et puis une deuxième, une troisième…

Mélusine écoutait, bouche bée, comme effrayée.

— Un jour, sans même vous demander pourquoi, vous avez commencé à douter. Rien de plus normal, c'est instinctif chez l'humain. Un de ces soirs, alors qu'il était rentré toujours un peu plus tard et pendant qu'il prenait sa douche, vous avez cherché dans son portable. Vous ne saviez pas ce que vous vouliez trouver mais c'était plus fort que vous. Et vous avez vite compris que ces fameuses soirées entre potes avaient un petit accent latin, qu'elles mesuraient environ un mètre soixante-quinze, brune, cheveux longs et que ces « soirées » s'appelaient en fait Melinda.

Damien tira la dernière bouffée. Médusée, Mélusine n'eut la force que de faire un simple pas vers lui. Après de longues minutes, elle se mit à crier :

— Espèce de salaud ! Espèce de salaud ! hurla-t-elle se précipitant vers le bord du pont. Tu es un de ses copains de beuverie, hein ? C'est ça ? Il t'envoie parce que l'Espagnole l'a largué et qu'il regrette ses conneries ? Pauvres types… Toi et lui : deux pauvres cons !

Damien restait de marbre. Il écrasa son mégot sur le sol.

— Comment tu sais tout ça, hein ? Il s'en est vanté ? Il t'a donné des détails ? Non ? Mais je vais t'en donner moi des détails sur son comportement… Tu vas voir : je vais l'habiller pour l'hiver ! Et l'Espagnole avec, cette salope !

De chaudes larmes recouvraient les pommettes saillantes de Mélusine, rougies par le froid.

— Je suis vraiment trop conne, conclut-elle, la colère retombant légèrement.

Damien se dressa face à elle.

— Ni un de ses potes, ni même une connaissance. Je suis là pour toi, pas pour lui. Et comme je te le disais, je reviendrai ici te voir, au même endroit, chaque lendemain à minuit et demi précis s'il le faut ! Jusqu'à ce que je sois certain que tout cela est derrière toi. Que ça devienne du passé enfoui, là au fond de ton cœur, que tu en oublies la plupart et que tu ailles de l'avant.

Mélusine releva le visage. Elle regarda Damien droit dans les yeux.

— Tu es qui alors pour savoir tout ça ? Vas-y, explique-toi ! interrogea-t-elle plus calmement.

Damien jeta un coup d'œil vers la nuit étoilée. Sans réfléchir, Mélusine fit de même. La pleine lune illuminait leurs fronts.

— Tu te souviens de ton jumeau ?

La question sembla asséner le coup de grâce. Les jambes de Mélusine tremblaient, fragiles comme celles d'un nouveau-né.

— T'en souviens-tu ? insista Damien.

— Evidemment que je m'en souviens… Enfin, non je ne m'en souviens pas mais je connais toute l'histoire ! répondit-elle.

— Demande à ta mère qu'elle te donne son vrai prénom. Pas celui de sa naissance qui figure l'état civil, son vrai prénom : celui qu'elle voulait lui donner si…

Damien s'interrompit.

— Tu es fou ! A cette heure, appeler ma mère ? Elle va faire une attaque ! lança Mélusine inquiète.

— Fais-le, reprit Damien.

Ne sachant pas réellement ce qu'elle devait faire,

Mélusine fouilla dans son sac. Elle chercha mécaniquement le numéro de sa mère dans le répertoire de son portable et appela avant de perdre courage.

— Maman ? Oui c'est moi… C'est moi Mélusine ! Oui, oui tout va bien, ne t'inquiète pas…

— *Qu'est-ce que tu veux ? Tu as vu l'heure qu'il est !* répondit une voix enrouée.

— Oui, je sais… Ecoute-moi, c'est important : quel est le vrai prénom d'Arthur ? demanda Mélusine empressée.

— *Quoi ? Qu'est-ce que tu racontes ?*

— Arthur, mon jumeau ! Quel est son véritable prénom ? Enfin je veux dire : comment tu voulais l'appeler si…

Mélusine baissa la tête et se couvrit l'autre oreille.

— Je t'entends mal… Parle plus fort !

— *Mais enfin Mel, qu'est-ce qu'il te prend de me demander une chose pareille au milieu de la nuit ?*

— J'ai besoin de savoir ! Bon sang, ce n'est quand même pas la mer à boire ! Qu'est-ce que ça peut faire après toutes ces années ? dit-elle en haussant le ton.

— *Avant votre naissance, ton père et moi avions décidé de vos prénoms à tous les deux. Tu es née la première et nous t'avons donné « Mélusine ». Ton frère est arrivé quelques minutes après toi… sans vie.*

— Je sais tout ça, je sais ! Alors ?

— *Etant donné les circonstances, nous n'avons pas eu le courage de lui donner le prénom que nous avions choisi… Et il fallait quand même lui donner un nom car il était né. « Arthur » est arrivé comme n'importe quel autre aurait pu être choisi. Nous étions si heureux de te voir respirer et brisés de le tenir inerte. Ton frère aurait dû s'appeler Damien.*

Mélusine laissa tomber son téléphone sur le pont. Elle releva les yeux pour chercher Damien du regard. Le trottoir était vide. Elle fit volte-face mais elle était seule. Sur le sol, devant ses pieds, la fumée du mégot de cigarette s'essoufflait peu à peu. Dans son esprit, la voix de Damien résonnait encore comme le son d'une mélodie apaisante :

— *Je reviendrai ici te voir, au même endroit, chaque lendemain à minuit et demi précis.*

A Scoop of Henry
CHERYL MCALISTER

Carol stood on the Pont de la Tournelle staring at the back of Notre-Dame. She removed the lid from the heavy cardboard box and was astonished to find the plastic bag containing Henry's ashes secured with a common twist tie. She untied and pocketed it along with a small slip of paper that read: Henry Delaunay, beloved husband, April 6, 1934 to August 16, 2014.

This was the first time Carol had looked at the ashes. How could this be all that was left of the man she had loved? Where was his beautiful silver hair, his blue eyes, his kind heart? She began to cry, making a gray blur of the river, the cathedral and the sky.

Last year, when she promised Henry she would pour his ashes into the Seine, she hadn't believed she would have to go through with it. Men can live for years with prostate cancer, but not Henry. He had refused surgery, saying he didn't want to live with the consequences of the operation. At least you'd be alive, Carol thought. But as usual, she hadn't argued.

Now she wiped her eyes, opened the bag and raised the box when a whistle shrieked.

"Arrêtez, Madame!" called a young policeman striding toward her. *"Que faites-vous?"*

Despite 50 years of living with Henry, a high school French teacher, Carol hadn't learned much of the language, but she understood the policeman's question.

"I'm um… Mon mari… Il est dans la boîte. Il est écrémé."

"Your husband is in the box, and he has had the fat removed?" He looked at the contents of the plastic bag in the box and understood. "Ah," he said, *"Votre mari était incinéré, et vous voulez verser ses cendres dans la Seine, n'est-ce pas?"*

All Carol understood of the sentence was *n'est-ce pas*, so she used her usual response when in doubt, *"Oui."*

"Non."

"But I promised."

"Désolé, Madame, this is against the law."

"Please, officer."

"Allez, Madame. Circulez, move along, *s'il vous plaît."*

Carol looked at him in disbelief. Surely other people had had their ashes spread in the Seine. Why not her Henry? But the cop was adamant, and he stood guard as she closed the box and hurried off the bridge toward their rental on the rue Poulletier.

She shouldered open the heavy blue door and entered the courtyard only to be stopped by *Madame* Gilbert. Carol knew the entry code so she hadn't had to deal with the effusive concierge when she arrived early that morning.

"Ah, *Madame* Delaunay, welcome. But where is *Monsieur?"*

Madame Gilbert adored Henry. He could gab with her for hours over a cup of tea and her special *madeleines*. But in 16 years of renting the lovely ground floor apartment on the île Saint-Louis, Carol had never warmed to the plump little woman and had never tried her baking.

Carol looked at her, unable to speak, and *Madame*

Gilbert understood immediately.

"*Oh ma pauvre. Oh là, là, là, là. Venez, venez,*" and she threw her meaty arm around Carol's bony shoulders and guided her inside.

Carol hadn't even unpacked. Her small suitcase sat upright with its telescopic handle extended beside the white couch.

"*C'est tout ce que vous avez amené?* This is all you bring?"

"*Oui*," said Carol.

"You don't stay long?"

"Um, I don't know."

"*Ah, vous êtes toujours choquée. Laissez-moi faire.*"

"*Oui*," said Carol. Then, "*Choquée*, oh, you mean shocked? Yes, I suppose I am."

Soon Carol was sitting on the couch sipping tea. Henry was on the black lacquer coffee table, the one he used to rest his feet on, and *Madame* Gilbert was arranging *madeleines* on a plate.

"I'm sorry, *Madame* Gilbert, I'm not hungry."

"*Non, non,* you eat, *Madame. Vous êtes maigre,*" she fluttered her hands, "like a bird."

"*Oui,*" said Carol.

"Now, you tell me, please. What happen?"

Carol told her everything, even how the policeman shooed her off the bridge. After both women cried, Carol took a tentative nibble of a *madeleine* to be polite. It was delicious, and she quickly ate it.

In her eagerness to serve Carol another, *Madame* Gilbert knocked the box of Henry's ashes off the table. When it hit the floor, the cover popped off, and a puff of gray-white powder blew out and settled on the rattan rug.

"Henry!" Carol cried, lunging for the box.

"*Non, non, c'est bon.* Henry like it here. He is good in the rug."

"But someone will vacuum. He won't be there forever."

"Then we put some in the *jardin*." *Madame* raised her arms. *"Et voilà,* this how you keep your *promesse! Vous saupoudrez Monsieur* a little bit all over Paris." She made a sprinkling motion with her fingers.

"But how? I can't bring myself to touch him—I mean, his ashes."

"Moi non plus, I don't want to touch. *Mais attendez,"* She got up, rummaged in a drawer, and returned with a long handled plastic coffee scoop that she placed atop Henry's box.

The two women sat for a moment staring at the scoop before collapsing in laughter.

The next day Carol put Henry's box in her shopping bag and set out for the Eiffel Tower. She and Henry hadn't visited it in decades, but she knew it would be crowded and a good place to practice sprinkling. She chose a spot near the base of one of the legs, beside the stairs to the restrooms, and sprinkled one scoop. Carol looked around to be sure no one was watching. For once, she was glad to be old and invisible.

From the Eiffel Tower, she walked through the Champs de Mars, but the long stretch of grass in the park seemed too exposed to sprinkle Henry without detection, so she chose a bench under one of the manicured trees. Checking the contents of her bag, Carol discreetly scattered him on the ground beneath the bench. Later, she re-tied her shoelace at the main entrance of the Grand Palais and left a scoop of Henry in the grass.

She couldn't resist visiting the Petit Palais to peruse the nineteenth-century collection. Sorry Henry, Carol thought, for once you have no choice. I'll take as long as I like, and you'll just have to wait quietly by my side. After lunch on the terrace of the museum's café, she deposited a scoop of Henry in the tropical garden.

At the Jardin des Tuileries, Carol decided it was too awkward to keep fumbling with the twist tie, so she put it in her pocket and folded the plastic bag that contained Henry's ashes.

Madame Gilbert was waiting for Carol to return and invited her to share a pot of tea and a plate of butter cookies. Carol was tired, but curious. So this was where Henry came in the afternoons while she read or knitted alone in their apartment. Carol had always been welcome, but she would have felt awkward just sitting there while Henry and *Madame* chatted in French. It wasn't as if she hadn't tried to learn French over the years, but she couldn't get a sentence out without Henry correcting her. In the end, she quit trying. And who knew *Madame*'s English was so good?

"*Et bien,* how did it go?" *Madame* asked.

"*Pas mal,*" said Carol. "But there's a lot left."

Madame Gilbert lifted the box off the table to test its weight. "Perhaps you leave two or three *cuillères* at each place, *non?*"

"*Oui.*"

After this, the two ladies chatted about other things. Carol learned they had both been high school teachers: *Madame* Gilbert taught science and math; Carol taught art. Both loved gardening, both were knitters and both were widows. By the time Carol walked back to her apartment, it was dark.

The next morning was cold and drizzly. Carol, still weary from her excursion the day before, decided to stay closer to the apartment. She would make only one stop, at Henry's favorite restaurant, the Brasserie de l'Isle Saint-Louis. The problem was where to leave a scoop of Henry. There was only sidewalk outside, and inside she would be seated beside strangers at one of the long café tables. She couldn't sprinkle Henry on the rug, could she? Someone would surely see. She would have to figure it out when she got there.

The staff was always happy to see her jovial husband,

and if the owner *Monsieur* Paul were there, he would join them for a chat. But Carol knew busy waiters could be curt, and she was afraid they might be rude to her now that Henry wasn't there to charm them. Nevertheless, she gathered her courage and her box of Henry, and made her way to the brasserie. She arrived a little past 1:30 p.m., hoping most of the lunch crowd would have left. It was still busy, but *Monsieur* Paul spotted her from behind the bar and rushed over to embrace her.

"*Madame Delaunay, bienvenue!* But where is *Monsieur?*"

Carol's eyes filled with tears as she told the story of Henry's passing.

"*Je suis très désolé,*" said *Monsieur* Paul. "Here, *Madame,* please sit here. Lunch is on the house."

"Oh no, I couldn't."

"*Non,* I insist."

Carol placed her trench coat and the bag with Henry's box on the seat opposite her. In the past, Henry had always ordered for her. Now, for the first time, she said, "*Steak-frites, s'il vous plaît.*" It was Henry's favorite, and when she had finished, *Monsieur* Paul brought a coffee for her and one for himself.

"How wonderful that you come back to Paris," he said as he sat directly on the bag with the box in it. "*Oh, pardon,*" he said jumping up amid a puff of powder. "It seem I have crush your box of flour."

Carol jumped to retrieve her shopping bag. "*Oh pas problem,*" she said. "I'll just put it under the table." She glanced in, replaced the cover on the slightly crushed box and sat again with Henry's remains secure between her legs. "So how are your sons, *Monsieur* Paul?"

That evening, she could barely get the story out to *Madame* Gilbert, the two women were laughing so hard.

On Sunday, Carol ventured to the Bastille market to buy flowers and a dessert for *Madame* Gilbert, who had invited her to dinner. Henry had loved to stroll the stalls of the market and always bought a roasted chicken for their Sunday dinners. The market made Carol nervous— more so over the past several years as the vendors and clientele had become more and more foreign. Nevertheless, it was the perfect spot to sprinkle Henry.

Despite the intermittent rain, the market was crowded. Parents pushed strollers, shoppers lugged bags, and tourists stopped to ooh and ah. Carol shopped the way Henry always did, strolling up one long alley and down another, comparing prices. She stopped at a flower stall and bent to smell the gorgeous apricot roses. At that moment, someone snatched her bag and ran to the right while another man grabbed her backpack purse and tried to run in the opposite direction. But Carol had buttoned the straps of the purse under the shoulder pads on her trench coat to keep them from slipping. The purse-snatcher pulled her over backwards before he panicked and let go.

"My bag!" she cried, struggling to rise. The first culprit had dropped it, and Henry's ashes were strewn all over the aisle. Carol watched helplessly as the ash clung to the damp soles of the Parisians' shoes. A smartly-dressed, middle-aged woman finally picked up the trampled bag and returned it to her.

"My fertilizer," Carol lied. "*Merci.*" The box was crushed, the plastic bag inside was about a third full, and ashes covered the bottom of the tote.

The fishmonger, an Arab man with a large moustache, gave Carol a bag of ice in case she was injured, and the lady from the flower stall brought her a bouquet of the apricot roses.

"Let me pay you," said Carol, but the woman refused her money.

The fishmonger said, "You rest here. Then I take you home."

"Absolutely not," said Carol, trying to reassert her

dignity by swiping at the dirt on her coat and pants. "I'll take the Métro."

"*Bon*, I take you."

"No," she said, "I have to buy a tart."

"Ah, you want *tarte?* Good." He walked Carol to a pastry stall where she bought a Mirabelle tart that he arranged in her shopping bag along with the "fertilizer" and the bouquet of roses. Then, he took her arm and turned toward the Métro.

"Really, I can go myself," Carol said.

But the man would hear nothing of it and walked her all the way through the turnstile and onto the platform. When the train arrived he shocked Carol further by kissing her on each cheek.

Madame Gilbert sat dumbfounded as Carol recounted her story over dinner. "You know, *ma chère*, you are much more *intéressante* than your husband, *que Dieu le bénisse*. How much of *Monsieur* did you lose?"

"Lots, but some spilled in my tote. How will I get it back in the plastic bag without touching it?"

"We do *dans le jardin, hein?* If some spill, it go in the dirt."

The next morning, Carol met *Madame* Gilbert in her garden. *Madame* had a pair of yellow rubber gloves for each of them. She tapped the ash out of the tote and into the plastic bag Carol held open. Both women turned their noses to avoid sniffing up any Henry.

When the cloud of ash settled, Carol looked into the shopping bag. "It's sticking to the inside."

"*Pas de problème*, is plastic. We wash with… how you call this?"

"A hose?"

"A ose?"

"No, a HHHHH-OSE."

"*Bof, c'est un tuyau d'arrosage*. You say this."

"Twee-o d'arrow-sage."

"*Non, tu dis a*RRRRR*osage*," said *Madame* rolling her Rs in the back of her throat.

Carol tried again, "Arrrrrrosage."

"*Très bien!* You see? Your French is better than my English."

"Really, Anne-Marie, you know that's not true!" But Carol loved the compliment.

Madame pinned the shopping bag to her clothesline to dry, and Carol took the box of ashes back to her apartment.

"Henry, you're on your own today," she told it. "Anne-Marie and I are going to her favorite knitting store in the ninth."

Carol took a few days off from Henry; she needed time to recover from her ordeal, but she was also having a wonderful time running errands with Anne-Marie. Although she had seen most of the city with Henry over the past 50 years, they had visited more or less on its surface. Now, thanks to Anne-Marie, Carol was seeing it as a Parisian, and she was surprised to find she loved it.

One evening, Carol accompanied Anne-Marie to a neighborhood potluck around the block from their building. Carol was touched when Anne-Marie introduced her as an old friend.

"*Vous êtes très bienvenue,*" said *Monsieur* Zahir, the Afghani antique dealer who organized the party, as he handed Carol a plate of chicken with saffron rice.

"I feel welcome. *Merci beaucoup.*"

"Carol, *comment vous appelez cela?*" asked Anne-Marie's friend, Mathilde, holding up a cookie.

"A chocolate chip cookie."

"*Délicieux! Vous me donnez la recette?*"

"The recipe?" asked Carol. "*Oui!*"

"*Madame* Delaunay, how long you stay in Paris?" asked *Madame* Zahir.

"I don't know." She looked at the neighbors sharing

food and chatting under the streetlamps. Anne-Marie was serving cookies to a cluster of eager children. "I'm very happy here," she said.

Nights were still difficult, though. Carol missed the sound of Henry's breathing in her ear and his arm tucked around to keep her warm. After yet another sleepless night, she gave up and climbed out of bed at 5 a.m. She puttered around the tiny apartment, but at 6 she decided to go for a walk with Henry's box by the Seine. It was time to start sprinkling him again, and there was little chance of meeting a policeman on the bridge; at that hour, the only people on the street were the garbage men and the street cleaners. She pulled on her trench coat, wrapped a turquoise scarf—a gift from Henry—around her neck, picked up the box of ashes, and headed back to the Pont De La Tournelle.

On the bridge, she removed the cover from the box and unfolded the plastic bag. She turned halfway around to look for cops. She only intended to sprinkle one scoop of Henry in the river, but it seemed best to make sure she was truly alone.

Carol marveled at the red, orange and purple clouds to the east, and when she turned back she found the cathedral ablaze in golden light against a deep cerulean sky.

"You were right, dear. Paris is a splendid city." She turned to her left, but bumped the box of ashes, sending it over the side of the bridge.

"Shit!" she gasped, grabbing for the box. But it was too late. The box had bounced off the ledge below the guardrail, and the bag and the scoop had flown out. She watched as they hit the river. The box floated, but the baggie soon filled with water. The ash trailed out of it in a thin line on the surface.

Carol smiled, despite the tears that traced the wrinkles in her cheeks; her promise was fulfilled.

"Goodbye, my love," she whispered. Then she turned and walked home to the rue Poulletier.

Love Unlocked

ADRIA J. CIMINO

Summer 2014

My flyers littered the bridge that I only wanted to protect. I chased after them as they fluttered out of careless hands and danced with the wind. For the better part of a week, I had stood on the Pont des Arts in front of the massive load of padlocks weighing down its frail skeleton.

"Do you know that when you attach one of those locks to the bridge, you're violating it? Read this, and you'll understand." But not many people wanted to understand. They didn't want to read my carefully prepared document detailing the structural and environmental damage caused by the locks. They were only interested in writing their names on locks and fastening them to the bridge's railings to attach their love story to the story of Paris.

In the best scenario, my audience had ignored me. In the worst, they had doused me with water and told me to go fuck myself. My gentle tactics clearly hadn't worked. So after days of putting up with verbal abuse, it was time to be bold. I returned to the bridge at dusk and attached myself to it with my bicycle chain. A few people giggled, and others looked shocked. But, in all the hours I had spent on that bridge, this was the first time no one dared to fasten a lock... or even approach the railing.

Except one person. I saw him out of the corner of my eye. By now, night had fallen and my tired eyes scanned the pages of a classic I promised myself I would read before classes started in the fall. He seemed to be looking for something amid the layers of locks, and he was so absorbed in his search that he stepped on my foot. My toe now seemed as bright as the chipped, red nail polish I should have removed days ago.

"Excuse me!" he exclaimed as I let out a cry. "I didn't see you there."

"Forget it. I'm fine. What are you doing anyway, fiddling around there over my head?"

"Looking for a lock."

"Are you kidding? Do you actually think you're going to find some old lock in that mess of metal?"

"I think I remember where we put it..."

I shook my head and gazed through the misty gas-lamp light illuminating the river. Upside-down images of buildings and trees cast dark spots along the edges. And then there were the locks. Dark chunks of ugly metal growing across the bridge like aggressive tumors.

"You're a part of this, then," I said.

He stopped and looked down at me. For the first time, I saw his face. Beautiful on one side, marred on the other by a jagged scar. Like the bridge. I lowered my gaze for an instant. Enough time to mask the surprise.

"It's not like I put up every lock on this bridge!" he said. "You don't have to be so accusatory. You make it sound as if I'm in a conspiracy against mankind or something!"

"Fuck you... and all of you who hide behind

everyone else! It's easy to say you weren't the first and to follow the crowd. That way, no one takes responsibility. Instead, you get defensive and then yell at the person who says what you don't want to hear. I know. I've seen that kind of shit all week."

"You've been here all week?"

"Chained, no. Unchained, yes. Chained worked better than unchained."

He lowered himself to the ground beside me, continuing his search and talking at the same time.

"How long are you going to stay here? Chained, I mean…"

"Well, I guess I'll eventually have to pee or take a shower. I didn't plan it out… I just needed to make this statement, to do something."

"Found it." His words were filled with both satisfaction and regret.

"OK, you found your lock. Now what? Are you going to, like, take a picture with it or kiss it? I discourage the kissing. Too many hands have touched those locks."

He smirked, yet his eyes, now nearer to me, seemed sad. They looked almost golden in the dimness.

"I'm unlocking it." He pulled a small key out of the pocket of his jeans, released the lock and tossed it into the trash can a few feet away.

"Why did you do that?"

"Our story is over. We broke up today."

"You only wanted to get rid of your lock because the relationship is over? Typical. You're not doing this because you care about the bridge or our environment."

"Typical of what? Of everyone except you? Of everyone who cares more about relationships and people than inanimate objects and vague ideas? You're a strange girl… uh… I don't know your name…"

I froze. I didn't need to have my personal life dissected by some stranger. Did I really want to tell him that I was an ordinary girl who grew up in a farmhouse an hour from the city? Did I want to say that, there, watching my grandfather work, I learned to appreciate well-built structures and natural resources? And did I want him to know that in spite of the poor outcome of my recent dates, I cared about relationships probably as much as anyone else? No, no and no.

And then, before I could decide whether to snap back or not snap back, two sets of heavy black shoes settled nearly toe-to-toe with my flip flops. I looked up and straight into the faces of the police officers.

Then came the list of questions I should have expected, should have been ready to answer. Instead, I had been so focused on making a statement that I hadn't thought of the consequences. And that is how I found myself being carted off to the police station just before midnight. The young man I had been speaking with was no longer in sight.

I sat under the neon lights for I don't know how long. The outside of the station might have looked like the entrance to a dungeon centuries ago, but the inside was typical of a bland 1970s office with brown linoleum floors and stark white walls.

At least I had my book, but I kept reading the same passages over and over because I couldn't concentrate. Behind my poker face and nonchalant attitude, I was quaking with fear. It's not like I was used to being arrested. The most illegal thing I'd ever done was smoke a joint at my best friend's birthday party last year. This was decidedly new territory for me.

Finally, one of the officers I saw earlier called me into her office. I gave her the basics. Name? Anna Citron. Yes, I know it's funny that my last name means "lemon" in French. Age? 19. Yes, I know I'm lucky that I'm not a minor, and you don't have to embarrass me by calling my parents or guardians about this. Address? Rue Cardinal

Lemoine. And yes, I know that Hemingway once lived on that street. But I live in a different building, and I'm not a writer. Just a literature student and I'm not sure what I'm going to do when I graduate. What the hell were you doing, Ms. Citron? Protecting the bridge, which is more than any of you have been able to do.

The police officer sighed, shook her head and leaned across the table toward me.

"Look, we could have you spend the night here. We could make a big deal out of it. But considering it's a first offense, if you can control the attitude, we can go easy."

I nodded, not quite sure what I was agreeing to, yet it didn't seem I had much of a choice.

"First of all, Ms. Citron, we don't want to see you chaining yourself to bridges again. This will be on your record. If you want more control over the law, go into politics. Now, let me see what I can do about the fine…"

"Fine?" I raised my eyebrows and thought about my meager budget.

She retreated into a back room, giving me plenty of time to worry and do mental calculations that in many cases involved me skipping meals and hocking a few pieces of inexpensive jewelry.

After another hour under the neons, I was a free woman. Thanks to some stranger who convinced them not only to let me go, but to waive the fine. I recognized him, half beauty, half beast, waiting in the lobby. His name was Justin.

"Thanks," I mumbled. "How did you swing that one?"

We were back on the street now, walking in the direction of the Seine.

"My motorcycle accident happened right around the corner… I got to know a few of the officers over there pretty well."

"The scar?"

"Yeah, along my arm and down the leg too."

"When did it happen?"

"Two years ago, on my way to pick up Pauline."

"The girl you just broke up with?"

"She broke up with me."

"Well, too bad for her!"

"That's nice of you, but I doubt she sees it that way. I think, for a long while, she felt guilty about my accident and the injuries… and a relationship can't be built on guilt."

"It was wrong of you to say that I care more about inanimate objects!" I snapped at him suddenly. "If I did, I wouldn't be feeling sad for you right now. I just so happen to care about people and the environment."

"Wanna sit down?" he asked.

I sat on Justin's good side, seeing the smoothness of one cheek. We dangled our legs over the edge of the riverbank. From afar, we heard laughter, crying and conversations. The sounds of a city that never sleeps.

"Why did you get me out of there, anyway?"

"I was curious."

"About what?"

"You. A girl who would chain herself to a bridge…"

"You thought I was a freak."

"Initially. But then I changed my mind. So what's your story?"

"If you think I hate the idea of romance or resent those supposedly happy couples sealing their love through metal, you're dead wrong." My snappy voice was back.

"I'm not thinking anything in particular…"

"Romance is something completely different. But that's another subject. The point is, I walked along the Pont des Arts so many times a few years ago, before the locks disfigured it. My last photo with my grandma was on that bridge. She pretty much raised me, out in the countryside… She would take me to the city a lot during the summer. I guess it's hard to see things change, and to accept that, when all you want is for things to go back to the way they used to be."

Strangely, I didn't feel the discomfort that usually would have arisen after such a declaration. Instead, I felt almost a sense of peace.

Justin's hand touched mine on the cool stone. I didn't move away. I caught his eye and smiled for the first time since we met. Slowly, the sky had been transforming itself from dark to light, from monochrome to multicolored.

"Do you think you'll do it again?" Justin asked.

"You mean chain myself to the bridge?"

He nodded.

"Not alone."

Justin smiled at me and shook his head. And then the two of us walked toward the sunrise.

Cafés and Sidewalks

The Little Book of Funerals
LAURA SCHALK

You think it makes you look interesting to write in a notebook while you're sitting alone in a café instead of like someone who has no friends or acquaintances in this city—someone who doesn't know a single person to invite for an *apéritif*.

You use a fountain pen and a spiral notebook with thick creamy pages lined in pale blue. You pretend to be jotting down profound thoughts, but you are really transcribing the fruits of your eavesdropping, which has become compulsive.

Surely people will wonder what that interesting-seeming woman is writing, you think. What has she observed that sent her hand groping inside her leather bag for a pen? And they will want to talk to you, and maybe they will.

Café Martin is a good place for this, you decide, where someone might notice you and strike up a conversation. The tables are close together, and the clientele is verbose. These people are more prone to talking about themselves than tapping on or peering at electronic devices like the patrons do at Chez Irène next door.

At Café Martin, others accompany their anecdotes with sweeping hand gestures that rarely knock cutlery off the tightly packed tabletops, though you keep your elbows clamped to your torso, suppressing your sprawling American tendencies.

Today you settle at a two-top away from the sidewalk, under the awning but next to the sunlit tables which are popular with the lightly clad demographic: men and women in careful t-shirts who favor oversize sunglasses and angle their faces upward while talking. Tanning trumps etiquette at Café Martin; it's not necessary to look at your conversation partner here. Maybe your mother's strictures really were suburban bullshit, not applicable outside the borders of New England.

"Suddenly I'm like, 'Oh my God I think I made out with your father when I was seventeen,'" announces a blonde who looks to be in her mid-30s.

"You *said* that to him?" Her companion has a careless updo and a pale pink, glossy moue.

"No, no, I just thought it. They have the same last name, and his father's in industry all right."

"Did it make you more or less inclined to sleep with him?"

"I've been asking myself that question all morning. I couldn't decide last night whether it would be grotesque or hot to kiss two generations of d'Hautevilles."

You think "grotesque," and the other girl agrees.

The waiter sets down a small pot heaped with glistening cubes of fried bread, dusted with salt and *fines herbes* next to your second glass of Chablis. Your excitement causes you to miss several minutes of your neighbors' conversation.

When the pot is almost empty, you realize you have been licking your fingers after each cube dissolves in your mouth, and your wine glass is smeared with greasy fingerprints. The paper napkin under the glass has disintegrated. You furtively wipe your hands on your skirt.

"So what's the deal with Fred? I still think he's gay," says the blonde.

"Who cares? He's such a mama's boy he probably couldn't get it up with anybody unless his mother personally approved the candidate." Marie—you have decided her name is Marie though you haven't heard the women call each other by name—twists a frond of hair that has fallen over her shoulder, and jams it into the clip on the crown of her head. She looks tousled, ready to climb into or out of bed, which you suppose is the intended effect.

You are a lamprey, an empty sack, you decide, and ask for the bill.

"That's not interesting, it's weird," says Sophie on the phone that evening. "Why don't you just move back? You can house-sit for my in-laws until you find a sublet. They're on a Galapagos turtle rescue mission for the foreseeable future. You've got the settlement, and the rest of your mom's annuity. You could not work for awhile."

"Is that the world's worst pick-up line ever? *'I think I made out with your father when I was seventeen.'*"

"Conceivably. I don't recommend you try it. Have you been trying out pick-up lines?"

"No," you say in a small voice. "No, no, no, no, no."

"Come back," Sophie says. "It's OK to quit your job."

"I just got here," you say. "I'm still settling in. I was unsettled for the first few months."

"Okay, but you don't need to be a martyr. At some

point, settling in has to become living a normal life. Working twelve hours a day and talking to your friends on another continent for human companionship doesn't feel like that to me."

You can't explain to Sophie how horribly afraid you are. You won't describe your conviction that if you give up and run away, you'll never achieve anything and be condemned to exist purely through mirroring others' experiences until you die. You can't go back, you think, after having lived abroad, gotten your work visa and your foreign apartment and your nominative contract with France Telecom. It's a small achievement in the grand scheme of things, but an important one in the scope of your life.

You think the beep-beep in your ear is a problem with the connection, but it's Sophie's call waiting. She apologizes, and says she needs to take the call. She offers to ring back, but you say you are about to go to bed anyway.

Your friend Carey has attended more funerals than anyone else you know. She is a font of good advice—on etiquette, attire, the appropriate length for commemorative remarks, what to carry in one's purse (an actual handkerchief and not Kleenex, breath mints, face powder.) It is permitted to smoke outside, in the parking lot for example, but not graveside. You need a good manicure—everyone will want to hold your hand.

You decide that co-hosting two memorials in six months makes you something of an expert yourself and that others could benefit from your acquired experience. The hand cream, the one-and-a-half medicinal glasses of wine before the proceedings commence, the most expensive control-top pantyhose: These are your own additions to Carey's playbook.

You start a special section in your notebook devoted to funerals, but not referencing your people who died.

It's difficult to eavesdrop on the couple sitting next to you. They don't speak much—to each other or to the newborn they've brought to the terrace of Café Martin. The baby is zipped into a fleecy sack in the thin sunlight. You resort to staring obliquely, through lowered lashes, which hurts your eyes after a moment.

The father tears into a large bloody steak. The mother strips all the flesh from a lamb shank, separating a tower of meat from the bone before forking the glistening filaments into her mouth. These parents exchange slow smiles when they pass the infant back and forth to each other. Occasionally, one or the other will get up and walk with the tiny thing when it wails. The baby's cheeks are the size of apricots and stippled with a bright red rash. Its arms make you think of macaroni for some reason.

A woman with brittle white-blonde hair eating alone a few tables away calls out gaily, "We've all been there! Oh it can be difficult when they're that age! Courage to you!" Reddish, crêpey skin hangs over her breastbone. Her bracelets clack on the tabletop.

A waitress stops, balancing a tray of dirty plates on her hip-bone, and says, "Ah, but once they sleep through the night the parents can go back to normal for a few years."

A middle-aged couple who have just sat down both laugh. The man rumbles, "Yes, you can be tranquil until they hit adolescence. Then you stop sleeping again, wondering what the little angels are up to and when they'll be coming home."

A whole conversation swirls around them. You clear your throat but can't think of anything to contribute. You consider the remains of your *salade parisienne* and poke a wedge of grayish hard-boiled egg with your fork.

"How are you holding up?" you ask Carey. You are calling to check on your oldest friend, whose father had a massive coronary and died in the Philippines last weekend. Carey has lost a sister, a step-father, a fiancé, and now her father; she is a veteran of mourning.

"Jesus Fucking Christ," she says. "You can't imagine the bureaucracy involved in shipping remains from one continent to another, even if it's a cardboard box of cinders weighing less than five pounds. In the end, we decided not to have a service at all. It was too much of a headache to figure out what to do with all the ex-wives and former step-children. And the fact that he left everything to the last one, that internet bride he was married to for five minutes, kind of impacted how we felt about our father's memory. His children will mourn him privately. No flowers. Donations can be made to my five-year-old's college fund, which is currently empty, thank you, Dad."

You hear a prolonged exhale, a puffing whisper, and picture Carey leaning out her kitchen window, blowing cigarette smoke into the airshaft.

"I guess I did wonder about the memorial," you say. You had had two competing visions, of Mr. Roberts' ashes resting on a mantelpiece in Manila, in a gaudy lacquer box; and of the first and the last wives standing side-by-side in the cemetery, wearing black veils and studiously ignoring each other as the pastor flung earth onto the coffin. You decide it would be impolitic to share your morbid curiosity, the scenarios you have penned in your notebook.

"I'm so, so sorry honey, it all sounds incredibly hard," you murmur. "I wish I could help in some way."

"I know, chicken, I know you'd be here if you could, but there's nothing you can really do. I've got the hubby and kid to distract me, and this tide of bile and pain will ebb one day on its own."

Carey is suddenly brisk. "Anyway, enough grim talk about my dreary reality. Tell me some amusing anecdotes about the good life in Paris so I can live vicariously. Have you seduced any charming Frenchmen this week?"

You admit that you have not seduced anyone lately, nor has anyone made an attempt on your virtue in recent memory. "It's tough to meet people at our age," you say lamely.

"Some of the classics still work," says Carey. "Put on a tight dress, go to a bar."

"Maybe they work in New York," you say. You are not sure about Paris.

"It's universal," your friend says firmly. "I want you to try it and report back to me. I'm serious."

You know how serious Carey can be, and begin evasive maneuvers. "I just loved the pictures of Chloe's dance recital," you say. "She looks radiant."

Perched on a banquette at Chantefable, an upscale bistro around the corner from your flat, a boy—maybe 5 or 6 years old? You can't tell, you're bad at judging these things—is on a special outing with his grandparents.

The waiter has taken away the remains of a plate of French fries. The boy is now making inroads on a dish of chocolate ice cream topped with a generous spiral of *crème Chantilly*. He has both ketchup and whipped cream smeared on his chin.

"I cried when Praline wouldn't wake up," he says. "Then I was angry."

"Praline was a good guinea pig, and she had a happy life, but pets don't live forever," says the grandfather sententiously. His napkin is tucked into the collar of his shirt.

"We will take Praline to the countryside this weekend, and you can bury her in the garden," says the grandmother.

Cochon d'Inde = guinea pig, you write, and you are proud that you know this.

"There are toads in the garden," says the boy. "Maybe Praline is scared of toads."

"Oh no, they will be company for Praline," says the grandmother, who is a symphony of gray—discreet pewter helmet of hair, silvery twin set, Hermès scarf. "After all, you are not afraid of toads. You're a big boy."

"I caught a toad, and it made pee-pee in my hand!" The boy bounces emphatically on the red leather banquette.

"*Ah non!*" exclaims the grandfather. "Toads do not make pee-pee or have terror-induced diarrhea in your hand when you catch them. They are secreting a bad-tasting substance to deter predators from eating them. It renders them unappetizing."

"If you had a mouth on your hand you could taste it!" cries the boy.

"Really, my dears, this is not a topic for the table," says the grandmother.

You twist the top back on your pen.

An Attempt to Explain the Paris Fandom
ANNA WEEKS

Paris. I am so overwhelmed I don't even know where to begin. I am generally a sarcastic person, but somehow, when it comes to Paris, sarcasm seems wrong. Oddly, everything serious I write makes me sound like an insane fangirl. If Paris were a leading Hollywood actor, it would be Brad Pitt, Tom Hiddleston and Chris Evans all rolled into one. Beautiful, romantic, and somewhat unbelievable.

Why the infatuation? Maybe because Paris is the one thing that has never disappointed me. Paris is as spectacular in real life as it is in your dreams. That's quite a distinction, don't you think? What other piece of your life has that kind of spotless reputation?

More specifically, Paris is beautiful. Its architecture and monuments are so rich, yet somehow they are squeezed into this tiny space, making them all the more impressive for their dense concentration. Even a great city like New York doesn't constantly assault your senses with so much beauty. And it's not only the architecture and the façades of the buildings. The interiors are just as lavish.

See. There I go. *Fangirling.*

But Paris not only has beauty, she also has brains. Would you like to see priceless pieces of art by the great movers and shakers in human history? Easy. How about expansive gardens and parks that make you glad you're alive to see them? No problem. Oh, you're interested in history and would like to relive it on the actual ground where it took place? Right this way.

You get the idea, and I know you've heard this all before. Still, it's not just these commonplace miracles that make Paris so special.

The best parts of Paris, like anything close to your heart, are the little things. Lovers on park benches. Corner cafés overlooking quiet, picturesque streets. Somehow, even everyday annoyances are touched by magic, making them charming and easier to bear. And if the annoyances are semi-mystical, day-to-day life becomes ethereal.

I know, I sound like a hippie on LSD. A hippie on LSD fangirling out, no less. Would you like an example? I am happy to comply.

It was 2008, and I was living in Paris. At 22, I was ecstatic. I couldn't believe I had beaten other applicants and landed a scholarship to study abroad. I had visited the city several times on vacation, but to *live and breathe* Paris for six months was a dream come true.

One afternoon, I witnessed the real magic of Paris. I was out for a leisurely stroll, so as to enjoy the lovely spring day. I meandered down an uncrowded avenue, glancing in the windows. It being Sunday, the shops were closed, so I took my time and appreciated life. Smelled the metaphorical roses.

My pace wasn't quick, but I was still going to overtake a gentleman who also appeared to be window-shopping. As I approached, I noticed him frequently glancing behind himself. It seemed odd, but–shrug–*pas de problème.*

I was getting closer and closer, and the next time he turned around, I noticed he was looking down. It seemed like he was waiting for someone to catch up. I followed his gaze. What do you think I saw?

Do you want to guess?

Not a dog, not a frog, not a house, not a mouse.

Not a boy, not a toy, not a moose, not a goose.

Give up?

It was a *bunny rabbit.*

This completely amazing Parisian man was taking his pet bunny out for a Sunday stroll.

The monologue in my head went as follows:

Is that a rabbit? It *is* a rabbit. Aw, he's so cute and fluffy! Wait. Is that guy actually waiting for the rabbit to catch up? He can't be. No way, that's not a *thing*, you don't "walk" a bunny. Holy crap. Oh my God. I can't believe it. That rabbit is following him. It *is* his pet bunny! HE'S TAKING HIS PET BUNNY FOR A WALK HOLY OH MY GOD WHAT THAT'S SO ADORABLE AND AMAZING.

Toward the end of my thought process, I was basically squealing inside. Outwardly, I had a restrained smile on my face. I hoped it looked indulgent and admiring, appreciative and knowing. Most likely, I looked like a crazy person with an exceptionally red face and a painful grimace. I probably looked like I was having a mini-stroke. It's possible that I actually was, considering how much I had to contain myself in the moment.

All of this happened in the blink of an eye, as I got close enough to identify that it was, in fact, a bunny. Once I passed this delightful duo, I couldn't resist turning around to confirm that I actually saw what I thought I saw.

Yup. It was true. That man was walking his bunny.

After I let that wash over me for a block or two,

grinning like an idiot the entire time, I decided there was simply no way my day could get any better, so I headed home to cook dinner and relive the experience in my head.

Now, be honest. That's not what you expected, right?

Remember, this event took place back in the spring of 2008. Social media was going strong, but it wasn't as all-pervasive as it is now. At the time, it didn't occur to me to tweet about it or snap a photo for Instagram. Maybe I was behind the times, but even putting it on Facebook didn't cross my mind.

In fact, I felt quite the opposite. I wasn't ready to tell anyone about it yet. This was one of those special jewels that not everyone gets a chance to see. This was *it*–my proof that Paris is a magical, wonderful place. I selfishly wanted to savor this joy a little longer before I enlightened the rest of humanity.

Eventually, I did share the news. The only other reaction I remember is the one of my best friend. Her response to the story was the way I reacted in my head while in the moment—she just did it on the outside. This gave me third-party confirmation that my experience could be categorized as out-of-this-world amazing.

And that's really what I've been talking about this whole time. That is the essence of Paris. Sure, the experience was enhanced by the city as a backdrop, but it wasn't the Eiffel Tower that made my day. It was Paris herself. I feel confident that this moment couldn't have happened to me in any other location in the world. The Musée d'Orsay, the Pont Neuf and the staircases up to Montmartre are beautiful and dreamy, but they merely set the stage for the best Paris has to offer—Bunny Rabbit Walks.

The Glove

APRIL LILY HEISE

Where was he?

My frosty sigh hovered in the thick January air. I checked my phone again. Zero missed calls, 15 late minutes—not great odds. I shuffled from side to side, a stiff arctic jig to unthaw my Popsicle toes. I really should have worn footwear more suited to the level of the thermometer. However, I thought I'd agreed to a leisurely stroll around the neighborhood, not a waiting marathon in front of the Anvers Métro station on this grisly afternoon.

A new trickle of passengers slowly climbing the subway steps, gliding through the fog of their united glacial breaths, lifted my spirits. I caught sight of a few blond heads emerging from the mist—well, I assumed he was blond. I forced a precipitous welcome smile in case he was the owner of one of these. However, none returned my *petit sourire*, inciting my chapped lips masked in Chanel rouge to curl back into a frown.

Another icy exhale. That was it. This was the last time I'd agree to my sister's virtual matchmaking. Or rather, attempts at pimping me out to her husband's friends as a Paris-friend-for-a-day (or night).

"But he's really cute!" she'd said, struggling to clinch the deal. She'd said the same thing a few months back when I got stuck showing around yet another of his seemingly endless best high-school mates passing through Paris on a European tour. Cute or not, that didn't change the fact that these guys all lived in my sister's adopted country of South Africa. Perhaps these set-ups were part of a secret ploy to get me to move there. Nevertheless, it was impossible to say no to her persuasive pleas. In the end, I'd given in again.

I'd reckoned it wouldn't do any harm to meet him for coffee—in the afternoon—and have a little neighborhood amble. It'd make my sister happy and earn some good karma. Right then, in my shivering state, I might have accepted to marry him on the spot just to escape this dismal Parisian winter. Each day had become grayer, the thermostat descending yet another few degrees, and our morales were almost as miserable as those who suffered through the Siege of Paris during the Franco-Prussian war.

I was getting antsy. Could he have sent a text message or e-mail while I was doing my desperate warmth-seeking foxtrot? I pulled my phone out of my pocket, stabbing at the screen with my gloved hand. Oh *merde*! I'd have to remove this source of precious warmth to punch in my passcode. What was worse? Suffering from frozen fingers or the nagging voice in my head repeating that I might have missed a call? With a tug of my right hand and a roll of my eyes, I reached my home screen. No little red #1 on my e-mail icon, no missed call from a *numéro inconnu*. *Rien*. My inboxes were as barren as the South African horizons.

Maybe I hadn't chosen the easiest place to meet, way up in the north of the city. While it was worth the trek, I'd extolled the many wonders of Montmartre mainly out of laziness. I'd just had to wander down from my bird's nest apartment perched high on la Butte to meet him. It'd taken me less time to get here than I'd been waiting. Geez, he'd only been here a day, and he'd already taken on the French habit of arriving fashionably late. I was all in favor of adopting local customs, but today was not the best day for this particular one. Not unless he wanted to meet me in the hospital's hypothermia unit or experience another form of Frenchness: the fury of an enraged *Parisienne*.

Maybe he'd misunderstood where we were meant to meet? I'd mentioned Sacré-Cœur in passing, yet I was planning to take him there after we'd defrosted in a nearby café with hot chocolate or *vin chaud*. Another wave of Métro-goers failed to produce any dreamy South Africans.

I looked despairingly up at the Basilica, regally crowning the mountain like a snowy fairytale castle. Is that where this prince was awaiting? One last glance at the empty Métro entrance and upward I shot. I'd zoom up for a quick look and could be back down in a flash.

I'd never run to God with such purpose or speed. Onward I raced, zigzagging through the sea of tourists browsing the tacky souvenir shops lining rue de Steinkerque. Surfacing from the masses, I paused to assess which staircase would get me up the slope the fastest and with the fewest human obstacles.

As I was about to launch upwards, my Himalayan hike was halted by a gentle tug on my sleeve. Spinning around, half expecting a sturdy rugby-playing Afrikaner, I was surprised by the smiling face of a tall, slender, well-dressed brunet. He raised a familiar-looking black glove. Mine, which I'd carelessly shoved into my pocket before my sprint.

"*Merci*," I blurted as I snatched it, immediately swinging back to my mission. This interruption threw me off and instead of taking the more direct staircase by the funicular, I charged past the *Amélie* carousel toward the series of lazily curving staircases that hug the gardens under Sacré-Cœur. A mistake soon signaled by the throbbing pain of under-exercised lungs after the second set of steps. What had I been thinking? It was insane to run up any set of Montmartre stairs; my silly choice of routes was a complete *folie*. By then it was too late. I was stuck halfway and had no time to lose.

I somehow reached the top without collapsing from lung failure. At least the horrific jaunt had warmed me up. Gasping, I scanned the *petite place* in front of the church. A quivering accordion player squeezed out a shaky tune. A young Spanish couple in fur-trimmed puffy parkas took selfies. A Polish tour group happily snapped shots of the city, oblivious to the frigid weather. No grazing blond springbok. Turning disheartened back toward the treacherous stairs, I froze midway. I hadn't come face-to-face with a suave fair-haired god at this religious summit. Standing a few feet away was my glove savior.

My embarrassed eyes darted out at the ashen rooftops. Had he chased me all the way up here? I doubted he'd come racing up just for the view, no matter how breathtaking. Sure, people probably practice for triathlons year-round, but he was hardly dressed for it. Athletic hypothesis aside, was he instead a Cinderella Prince Charming, the clear glass slipper replaced with my black leather glove? A sleazy gigolo straying from the seedy Pigalle sex shops a stone's throw away? Or was he simply a tourist bewitched by the magic of Paris?

I snuck a discreet glance. Refined Italian shoes, slim-fitting dark jeans, a smart wool coat and his own smooth leather gloves. He wasn't dressed like the average tourist. Perhaps he had just been an innocent local passing next to me when my pocket rudely spit out my glove?

I admired his distinguished Andy Garcia-esque looks with the same dark hair, parted in a wave skimming his ears. As I evaluated his age—possibly mid 40s—his eyes met mine. He smiled, nodding toward the foggy city as if to say, "Isn't she something?" I looked out at the endless architectural plains, interrupted by the occasional church tower and unfortunate 1970s tower block, and smiled back in agreement.

Our eyes locked for a millisecond. But I was supposed to be locating the missing South African. I broke our gaze, fleeing in renewed pursuit. Down the hill I swooped, not looking back and not being chased.

Arriving in front of the Métro entrance, my breathing slowly returned to normal. I shooed away any regrets—it was now too late.

A new wave of bodies ascended the concrete steps. This time they did produce the attractive blond I'd been expecting, almost half an hour late. He'd gotten lost.

Warming up in a nearby café, my mind couldn't help wandering from our get-to-know-you chat back up those picturesque but painful *escaliers*. Had I turned my back on fate and thrown spontaneity to the wind? This question often crosses my mind as I pass through the same Sacré-Cœur square, slowing my pace and wondering if I'll ever run into my lost *Prince Charmant* coming to collect my glove.

Paris is Good for Your Health

All the Wheat

BROOKE TAKHAR

I have never been to Paris. Don't cry for me though. I have smoked weed out of a hose bong with a 45-year-old drifter in Australia, almost fought a samurai on public transportation in Japan and waded (fully clothed) into the cerulean sea of South Beach in Miami.

So you could call me well-traveled. Cultured, even. But I still think my passport is incomplete without that inky smeared Parisian stamp. (I imagine it's a rotund croissant wearing a jaunty beret and expertly applied Chanel lipstick. My imagination is often stupid.)

Other than the iconic monuments, non-stop accordion street music and museums I would last 10 minutes in before getting hungry/bored/yelled at for taking pictures with my phone, the reason I absolutely *need* to go to Paris before my bones turn to dust is this: Parisian wheat.

To back up a bit, I have celiac disease. You can stop being sad—it's not a trendy killer. It just means when my intestines were on God's assembly line, they were accidentally perforated and subsequently slid onto the filthy floor. When nobody was looking, they were flopped back onto the conveyor belt and haphazardly smooshed into my mid-section. (That "angel" later went on to become Employee of the Month so you can guess I am more than a little bitter.)

Having celiac disease, I can't eat wheat or gluten. If I do, it's ugly. It's the variety of vomiting that you only hear echoing in frat house bathrooms. It's violent, often purple and leaves me sodden and weak for weeks. So, totally not worth it.

My good friend Karli, who speaks only the truth and has similar gut failures, took a risk on a hunch while in Paris. She gorged on croissants, pasta and baguettes—and she was FINE[2].

Whut. What. *QUOI?*

How have I not drained my child's college account to go sit on the banks of the Seine, surrounded by every baked good I have missed for the past several decades and systematically taken one bite of each? Pass the *crème fraîche, Monsieur.* I am here, and I am going to eat ALL THE WHEAT.

So then I started to think. If the wheat is magical in Paris, what else is possible on that delicious soil?

Could I actually do my 12 times tables sitting at a coffee shop with a breadstick tucked behind my ear?

Would I be able to do one real goddamn push-up on a cobblestoned street damp with the French air's invigorating morning dew?

Could I finally master a cat's-eye with eye liner under the soft glare of a Parisian bulb in a black-and-white loft overlooking a flat where topless male models drink espresso and do door-frame pull-ups?

---

[2] In case it wasn't abundantly clear, I am not a doctor. I don't even know any doctors. I can only speak to one person's experience with Paris wheat. Please don't take my advice. About Paris wheat or really anything at all.

WHAT ELSE IS POSSIBLE IN PARIS?
There's only one way to find out.

Les Urgences

DAVID WHITEHOUSE

The old man had fallen to the pavement, and his wife couldn't get him up. A passing woman, plump and middle-aged, had helped him to his feet and that was how I found the three of them, locked in a tight, immobile huddle in the bright light of a winter's afternoon.

"Are you going to be all right now?" the plump woman asked them.

The wrinkles on the face of the old man's wife were fragile like the threads of a spider's web.

"You'll be all right now, won't you?" the plump woman said.

The wife's eye shifted shyly through her wispy brown hair toward me. Encrusted with flaky skin, it was delicate as that of a young doe.

"I'm afraid I really couldn't say," she said.

I took the man's arm. He was big and burly with thick white hair. I glimpsed the seed of youth in the smile his wife directed at me.

The plump woman was gone.

"Dad! What are you doing? We're going to be late for

the PARTY!"

My kid, who I had fetched from school, was using a lamppost to swing himself round and round.

"Go on," the old man said. "Don't waste your time. You'll be late."

"Don't worry," I said. "We've got lots of time. We're early."

The three of us shuffled forward, the wife holding one of his arms and me the other. It was a hundred meters to his house, he said. But he couldn't keep going, and I caught him as he slumped down again. We got him back upright, but he could go no farther. We were stuck.

"DAD! I don't want to stand here in the COLD!"

"I'll call an ambulance," I said.

I pulled out my phone.

"Thank you," the man said.

The call was answered straight away. I told the woman where we were.

"His wife and I tried to get him home," I said. "But he can't walk any more. We're stuck."

"Is he inebriated?" said the voice on the line.

"What?"

"Is he in a state of inebriation? Is he drunk?"

"No," I said. "He's an old man."

"I'm eighty-five years old," the man said.

"He says he's eighty-five years old," I said.

"And he's not drunk?" the operator asked.

"No."

"I'll send an ambulance."

We waited, motionless. My child sulked. The man's wife, elegant in her long black winter coat, said nothing.

The ambulance arrived, along with a police car. Three young men jumped out of the ambulance. Two blue-uniformed women emerged sluggishly from the car. They wore black boots and carried long black truncheons. The old man's wife stood aside and looked at me, as if puzzled.

We were in Paris. I held the man up from behind by slipping my arms under his armpits.

"Good afternoon, sir," said the ambulance driver. "We've come to take you to the hospital."

"I'm not going to the hospital," the old man said. "I want to go home. It's a hundred meters down this street."

"If you want to go home, call a taxi," the young man said. "I can only take you to the hospital."

I was starting to sag under the old man's weight. The five uniforms stood impassive before us.

"I'm a bloody doctor," the old man said. "And so is my daughter. I want to call her. Her number is at home."

"It's best to be examined," I said. "Then you can call your daughter."

The driver of the ambulance folded his arms.

"Yes," he said finally. "You need to be examined."

"Maybe your wife can get your daughter's number?" I said. "While you get in the ambulance."

"Don't ask her," the old man said. "She's got Alzheimer's."

At this, the other paramedics moved forward and grabbed the old man's arms. The driver, arms still crossed, gave me a small nod. I stepped away. My child, like a wild horse springing out of a box, charged headlong down the street.

It started the next Sunday morning as a dull ache in my testicles and got worse. By the time I stood in my living room, in front of the parents of the new kids at my children's school, it felt like a spoonful of molten lead had been dropped into each one of my balls.

The parents had come round to discuss how we could share the job of taking our children to school.

Five assorted kids were running wild in the background. The visiting mother was a tall, large-breasted woman, and as the pain grew worse, I struggled to keep my chin up to meet her gaze.

"I'm a public relations consultant," she said. "So it's very difficult to know exactly where I will be on a particular day…"

"Stop leaning against the wall," my wife said to me. "Why can't you stand up on your feet?"

The husband shook his head and sighed, staggered by the dimensions of the problem. I wanted to cup my balls.

An intense round of negotiations followed. I smiled through gritted teeth. There were numerous complications. Mondays. Tuesdays. Wednesdays. Thursdays. Fridays.

I could feel a fever coming on. After what seemed long enough for the international war crimes trial of a minor African warlord, it was done.

"My balls hurt," I said to my wife once they had gone.

The emergency doctor came straight around, and we grappled briefly in the children's bedroom, my wife having indicated this was where the examination should take place. My temperature was through the roof.

"You should have gone to the hospital," the doctor said, "rather than calling me. If there's torsion in the balls, you have only six hours to save them."

"Six hours? To save my balls?"

My balls: six hours.

"When did they start hurting?" he asked.

"They've been hurting for… a few hours," I said.

The ambulance was soon there, and I was bundled into the back. Off we went, red light flashing, into uncharted territory. My amazing years of potency, it seemed, could be drawing to a spectacular end.

When I came back home it was possible that I would

be… something else.

At the hospital, a woman in a white coat pulled me out of the waiting room and took me to the guy that was going to examine me.

Except there was no guy.

How could there be no guy? She wasn't going to… it wasn't possible that… oh no.

I looked at her again, and three crucial points struck me. In this order:

1. She was wearing knee-high leather boots.
2. She was wearing black pantyhose. They had to be pantyhose, the alternative didn't bear thinking about.
3. A quick glance at her face showed her to be aged between 20 and 70 and free of any major disfiguring marks.

This was an infringement of my human rights. I would write to my health insurance company. I would complain to the association of balls doctors.

I would contact my Member of European Parliament.

I took my trousers off in the changing cubicle. Then I stepped into her office.

I lay down glumly on the couch.

"Please take your penis in your hand," she said.

She was wearing latex gloves. She rubbed a cold liquid on my balls. Then she ran a scanning device across them. She studied the results on a big screen in front of her. I could see now that she was about 50, wore glasses and had brown, mousy hair.

Her manner was quick and professional. This was crazy beyond my wildest dreams. My private little world had not been breached. She might as well have been a dentist. It might as well have been my teeth.

"There's no torsion," she told me. "You have a

minor case of epididymitis. You'll have to take some medicine."

"No torsion," I said. I struggled to absorb the news.

I was still me. I was going to leave here and end this day as I had started it.

"I just need to do one more test," she said.

She squeezed the skin on one ball between her fingers, and I screamed. She squeezed the other ball. I screamed again.

"That's right," she said. "Scream!" She grinned at me with a toothy leer. "Come on, SCREAM! Which one hurts the most?"

"Both of them!"

"Perfect," she said.

She laughed, and I roared in tortured relief.

At home I sagged triumphantly into an armchair. I was exhausted, but the medicine was already starting to wash the pain away.

"Dad! Dad!"

One of my kids came hobbling up to me.

"What?"

"My little toe is hurting. I think I need an ambulance!"

I called out to my wife.

"He says his toe is hurting."

"Just kidding, Dad," he said. And off he ran.

This story first appeared on Chippens.com.

Whine Country
APRIL WEEKS

The story begins in Germany.

I was living the dream—young, enlisted in the U.S. Air Force and stationed overseas at the largest military installation outside the United States: Ramstein Air Base, Germany.

The beauty of Ramstein is that it's approximately a four-hour drive from some of the greatest cities in Europe. Amsterdam, Munich, and yes, Paris were all at my disposal any weekend I cared to hop on the autobahn and take advantage of them. Unfortunately, living overseas also encouraged crazy family members and their even crazier friends to use me as a tour guide. Most of the time this was great fun, but sometimes it went terribly wrong.

It was a lovely July in 2008 when my sister Anna and her friend Karen embarked on a European getaway. My husband Steven and I welcomed them and encouraged them to use our house as a launching point to see all the sites of Europe. Since I didn't have a month's worth of leave, I left them to their own devices most of the month. But for their final hurrah, we planned a four-day trip to Paris. While Steven and I had been to Paris on numerous occasions, this was the first time my sister and her friend would be going.

Now Karen comes from a small town. A *very* small town. That, in and of itself, isn't a problem. The problem is that she *loves* her small town and is prone to homesickness. Looking back, saving the big hurrah for the end of the trip was Mistake Number One.

In 2008, the Fourth of July fell on a Friday. That meant Steven and I could savor a delicious four-day weekend without burning much leave time. What better place to celebrate America's independence than in France? After all, the French were instrumental in helping us gain our liberty from the oppressive monarchy situated just across the Channel.

Wednesday, 2 July 2008

The minute Steven and I got home from work, we grabbed Anna and Karen and loaded up the car. We hit the road at 6 p.m. and expected to arrive in the City of Light around 10 p.m.

Once we crossed the border into France (oh, the wonders of the EU—no passport control!) we were promptly flashed by a speed-control camera; my husband, a notorious speed demon, had been driving about 30 kilometers over the limit. It was one of the hazards of leaving the long stretches of unregulated German autobahn.

On previous trips to Paris, my husband and I had taken the high-speed train from Kaiserslautern, Germany to Paris in two hours. This was made extra magical because of the food and beverage car, which I *always* ended up in. Driving into Paris was a new and not-so-wonderful experience.

We planned to park near Charles de Gaulle airport and take public transport into the city. This plan failed when we missed the airport sign, the signs showing the distance to the exit, the exit—*all of it*. We searched, but were unable to find the mythical parking lot numerous co-workers had ensured would be there. We decided we would be able to navigate Parisian traffic and roads just fine. After all, we did it in Germany all the time. This was Mistake Number Two.

We reached Paris and the infamous roundabout circling the Arc de Triomphe. Even now, it's possible I died in a fiery car crash that evening and am actually living in some sort of weird limbo. Based on the way we drove, we most certainly should have died. We circled the Arc de Triomphe at least four times before veering off on what we thought was the proper road. Nope. BACK TO THE CIRCLE OF DEATH! We took the wrong street at least three more times while we desperately searched for our hotel. Tiny twisty streets with no apparent rhyme or reason, and somehow we always ended up back at that damnable circle.

We didn't make it to the hotel until 2 a.m. After a day at work, the drive down, relationship tests with the speeding camera, I told you so's, and near-death experiences, we were beat. We parked somewhere that appeared to be appropriate. This was Mistake Number Three. Blessedly, our room was still available.

Thursday, 3 July 2008

I figured after a nice rest, we would all be refreshed, over our crankiness and ready to hit the town. We woke up, had one of those delightful continental breakfasts that Europeans are famous for and prepared to do some heavy sightseeing. This was where *la merde* started to hit *le ventilateur.*

The four of us hopped on the Métro to get to the Louvre early, as you must if you want to take in the full wonderment of the museum without a glut of tourists ruining everything. I fully recognize the irony of that statement as I *was* a tourist, but I've never claimed not to be a snob.

Whenever I visit the Louvre, the first thing I visit is The Winged Victory of Samothrace. She's beautiful, sitting at the top of an elegant staircase in the former palace. If you can beat the crowds she's truly magnificent to behold. Armless and headless with a gorgeous wingspan, she is indomitable. Breathtaking.

I love the Louvre, but it's impossible to get out of. After three hours, Karen started to feel poorly. Maybe she needed to eat. She didn't *want* museum food, which was hard to come by anyway, so we made our way toward the exit. After an additional hour of fruitlessly searching for an exit (so many doors, but no way to get out), Karen exclaimed, "We're all going to *die* here!"

I kept thinking if she didn't shut her trap, she probably *would* die there, by my hand. Another hour later, with everyone's blood sugar dangerously low for group activities, we escaped from the palace into the warm French sunshine.

"Ah! Cafés!" I exclaimed. "Time for wine and baguettes!"

"No," responded Karen flatly. "I want something American."

Something American? In Paris? A bit of cordial bickering, and I gave in. It wasn't worth it. And we had reservations that night at Benoit, an upscale restaurant with a Michelin star rating. So for lunch, we ended up at McDonald's. MCDONALD'S. Crazy Americans. By this point, my frayed nerves were crying out for a glass of that amazing French wine, but I couldn't bring myself to do it at *McDonald's.*

"Okay!" I said, clapping my hands and wrapping up the remains of my greasy Royale with *fromage.* "Who's ready for Sainte-Chapelle?"

"I feel ill," whined Karen.

Of course you feel ill, we've just ingested the worst food this fine city has to offer.

"Suck it up, buttercup! You're in Paris! Let's do this," my sister responded helpfully. Grudgingly, Karen stood up, and we trekked to Sainte-Chapelle.

Sainte-Chapelle is gorgeous and peaceful, even when flooded with tourists. I figured we could all use a little peace and that would help Karen chill out, even if just a little. But amidst the soaring stained glass windows, Karen still seemed oddly agitated. When we finished she asked, "Can we go back to the hotel now?"

I sighed and let go of my plans to see the Musée d'Orsay that afternoon. Plans are meant to be altered, and after all, the morning was the best time to see museums. We'd do it first thing the next day.

Back at the hotel, Karen insisted there was something *really wrong* with her. She described her symptoms, and being a veteran of urinary tract infections, I diagnosed her. No wonder she was grumpy! I looked in the hotel directory for a physician. I was willing to pay for the doctor, if just to get to enjoy the rest of my visit.

"No," Karen said. "I don't want a doctor. I want to go back to the house."

"BACK TO THE HOUSE, IN GERMANY?!" I wanted to scream at her. Instead I said, "Let Steven get you some cranberry juice and a few bottles of water. I know you're feeling dreadful, but let's see if we can curb it a little. I'm sure the pharmacy has something over the counter for the pain."

I sent Steven on a mission for the medicine and beverages. He returned to the hotel not five minutes later.

"We've been booted," he said.

"Booted?"

"Yeah, the car."

"WHAT?!"

"I'm going to find out how to get the boot taken off, but someone else needs to go to the pharmacy."

It was getting later in the day, and I was starting to see red. So I decided to find the pharmacy myself. With the help of the front desk clerk and the friendliness of the Parisians (I say that without irony or sarcasm; Parisians, despite their reputation, are some of the friendliest people in the world.) I managed to track down an appropriate over-the-counter painkiller, cranberry juice and several liters of still water. Karen had demanded prior to my leaving, "Don't bring back sparkling water, April, it's disgusting. I don't know how these people drink it."

I returned triumphant, sure that everyone would make it to dinner and we would resume our regularly scheduled programming. Unfortunately, as I approached the hotel, I saw my husband still sitting near the car.

"Any luck?" I asked.

"Yeah, kind of. They should be here between now and tonight."

"NOW AND TONIGHT? What about dinner?" My voice edged toward a whine of its own.

"I don't know," Steven replied, sounding exasperated himself.

I sighed and trudged up the stairs to the room. My sister was doing her best to appease her difficult friend when I entered.

"I just want to call my mom. I'm not sure it's a urinary tract infection."

"Fine. Call your mom, but I got you this," I said. "I'm sure it will help."

"God, I hate cranberry juice. Are you sure about that medicine? I can't read the label."

"Yes. I spoke with the pharmacist. His English was impeccable. He assured me this would help with the pain. When we get back to the house I have antibiotics that will take care of the actual infection."

"I just want to talk to my mom."

"Then CALL HER!"

The phone conversation was tearful, and what I got from it was that perhaps Karen *didn't* have a urinary tract infection; perhaps what she had was a touch of homesickness.

The police and tow truck showed up in a remarkably timely manner, after only six hours, to remove the boot and take their fine, 300 euros. I was both pissed and elated because it meant we could still make our dinner reservations.

Despite my urgings to drink as much water and cranberry juice as possible and to take the damned medicine, Karen ignored me and continued to be in pain. But no way was I going to miss this meal. And my sister wouldn't either.

"C'mon Karen, it's going to be delicious and wonderful. Let's get dressed. Drink up, you're going to love it," my sister cajoled.

"No."

"Okaaaay…" I replied, at a loss on what to do with this 23-year-old child I suddenly had on my hands. "Well," I said, stretching out the 'l' for two seconds longer than I should have, "are you going to be okay in the hotel by yourself?"

"I guess," she said, followed with a sigh. "But I'd really rather go back to your house."

"In GERMANY?!" I responded, my voice taking on an edge. "Not tonight. We're going to dinner. We'd love for you to come, but the decision is yours."

"I'll stay, thanks."

The three of us left and enjoyed a sumptuous and remarkable meal at Benoit. Satiated, maybe a bit tipsy, I felt optimistic we would return to the hotel and find that Karen had taken the pills and drank all the liquids and our Parisian adventures could continue.

No such luck. We returned, and I noticed immediately that the pills were still in the box and she'd only consumed half a liter of water and zero cranberry juice. Still, I struggled to be polite.

"Feeling any better?" I asked. "Did you manage to rest?"

"Not really. I want to go back to the house."

"In GERMANY?! Let's see how you feel tomorrow. Drink up," I insisted.

"You don't want to miss *Paris* do you?" my sister asked. Silence.

"Okay, well, goodnight! Feel better."

Friday, 4 July 2008

"I want to go home," were the first words Karen said to me when I woke up.

"Karen, if you have a urinary tract infection, and I think it's pretty clear that you do, then getting in the car and driving for four hours is going to be much more unpleasant than staying here."

"No. I want to go *home*."

"To the STATES?! First, your flight leaves out of Frankfurt, second it's not for another five days, third, WE HAVE THE MEDICINE HERE TO TAKE CARE OF YOUR PROBLEM."

"I want to go HOME," she replied stubbornly. "I want to go back to Germany TODAY. I'm going to change my flight."

"But… but…" I'm rarely at a loss for words, but I no longer knew how to deal with this person. She had all of Paris at her fingertips, but wanted nothing to do with it. She couldn't be reasoned with. I looked to my sister and husband for help.

"C'mon Karen," my sister said quietly.

"No."

"Fine. Let me see if we can get a refund for the rest of the days we paid for." I left the room in a huff to talk to the hotel manager.

No refund.

The money, being mine and not Karen's, didn't seem to bother her. There was nothing left to do but pack up and head back to Ramstein. What's another 250 euros down the drain?

Back in the car, Karen's spirits improved incredibly. Also, miraculously she had no urge to pee the entire way home. Even more fantastically, once she changed her plane ticket (to leave Europe exactly one day early), she was in fine spirits. I suggested eating at a little German tavern in our village, but Karen wanted to go on base to Chili's. She never took my antibiotics.

I threw my hands up in disgust and told my sister, privately, that I was only making *one* drive out to Frankfurt—someone could take the train, I didn't care who it was. My sister, ever the trooper, spent her second-to-last day in Europe escorting Karen to Frankfurt International, about four hours round trip on the milk train, ensuring Karen got to her gate.

All I can say is she's a better friend than me.

Luckily, I would have numerous opportunities to visit and re-visit Paris during the rest of my stay in Germany. It's a beautiful and wondrous city. But for some, there's no place like home.

Note: Names have been changed to protect the guilty.

What's Love Got To Do With It?

Garden of Eden

VICKI LESAGE

As a mother of a 4-month-old girl and a 2-year-old boy, I've got one thing on my mind: cheating on my husband.

Not because my husband is two-timing (he's not). Not because I have a burning desire to horizontal-tango with a sexy stranger (I don't). But because an ad in the subway is telling me to (those bastards).

As I trudge up the Métro stairs to meet Papa for lunch, my daughter in the baby carrier and my son taking his jolly old time stomping on each step, the ad screams at me. I pause to catch my breath, brushing my disheveled hair out of my tired eyes, and fully take in the ad.

Seven apples stretch across the banner. Six days of the week, it declares, I'm a boring Granny Smith. But on Friday, glorious Friday, I could be a sexy, sassy Red Delicious.

"*Pomme!*" my French-American son shouts, proudly recognizing the fruit.

I'm half-tempted to shield his innocent eyes from the offensive poster. But since he can't read yet, I let it slide, mainly so I can investigate further.

The advertisement is for a dating website. Fair enough. For married people. Oh. Not cool. Not cool at all.

I'm shocked and offended on so many levels. And I'm not easily shocked or offended. I met my husband in a bar and have passed out on bathroom floors more often than I'd like to admit (or, to be honest, more often than I can remember). I'm no stranger to partying and livin' it up.

But I hold my marriage vows sacred. I promised to love my husband for better or for worse, or at least I think that's what I said during our French ceremony. Most of our conversations these days involve poop, farts or burps—either as conversation topics or background noise. But there's no one I'd rather clean up baby puke with.

I find so many things wrong with this billboard I hardly know where to begin. Just kidding. I'm a seasoned complainer; of course I know where to begin.

On a practical level, this can't be the best medium for their advertisement. Sure, cheaters take the Métro but everyone in Paris takes the Métro. Plenty of people outside the target audience—including my toddler—will pass by its content. Seems like an expensive way to reach a small percentage of the demographic. Maybe the ads would be more effective online? Or in a hotel restroom? Or the backseat of a taxi?

I'm irked that kids will see it because it endorses infidelity. Cigarette ads are banned so as not to encourage impressionable minds to pick up the habit. But cheating? That's OK because there's no smoking (at least not until *after* the sex).

And could they be any more clichéd? Seriously, a cheating website in France? Why don't they name the site SuperFrenchCliche.com? I'm surprised the ad didn't feature berets and baguettes. Way to feed into the stereotype, guys.

Their website (because of course I had to check it out) philosophizes, "How can you know the mistress/lover who's missing from your life if you haven't met?" Um, I didn't know I was missing that part of my life! It's bad enough that magazines and commercials shout at me to Lose the Baby Weight in Two Months and Banish Wrinkles and Eat Healthy, You Fat Lazy Slob.

Now I have to take on a lover, too? I just want to use the bathroom without a kid within arm's reach, and you want me to find a lover? A "mister?" (If that's not what a male mistress is called, it should be). Well, I hope my mister doesn't mind me falling asleep during the act because I'm running on empty.

How about instead of advocating extramarital affairs, they advocate fixing your marriage? Oh *pardonnez-moi*, that's not as (apple)saucy.

I'm appalled they presume I have time to search for a luh-va online. The internet is for reading *Homeland* spoilers and checking Facebook to see what my friends ate for dinner. While juggling an infant and slurping cold coffee. You must be joking if you think I have time to scan married dudes' dating profiles to find Mr. Right Behind My Husband's Back.

My biggest issue with this asshole of a website is it's an insult to those of us who struggled to find our partner in the first place.

After years of dating nice guys, bad boys and not-right-now guys, I finally found the man of my dreams. In Paris. A real live Frenchie. (Cue jaunty accordion music and romantic sunset over the Pont des Arts). It's the stuff movies are made of, right?

Maybe. But the path leading there was rough, and many a time I thought I'd die alone, except for my cats.

But I don't even have cats so I'd just die alone. (Cue sad accordion music and the pitter patter of raindrops on an empty cobblestoned street).

In my naïveté, I've always thought affairs happened by accident. A fan of drinking, I could see myself having one too many glasses of bubbly, meeting a mysterious stranger, and being tempted, in the heat of the moment, to forsake my wedding vows.

I wouldn't actually do it, mind you. My husband is the French Ryan Gosling but even better because I can kiss him without getting slapped with a restraining order (not that I tried to kiss Ryan Gosling, but that's only because I've never been close enough). In addition to being tall, dark and handsome, my husband volunteers for nighttime baby feedings, cooks a mean lasagna and massages the hell out of my feet. I'd be a fool to cheat on him.

But if it were ever to happen, being drunk out of my mind is the only way I could see it going down. A spur-of-the-moment lapse in judgment that I'd regret forever.

Not a premeditated internet search with a username and password.

How greedy can these cheaters be? Their private island isn't secluded enough? Their wallet is so full they can't close it? We hapless and hopeless romantics spend our lives looking for The One, and now these insatiable d-bags are searching for Another One.

The website has the right to exist, just like people have the right to scratch the seven-year itch. But, much like pistachio ice cream, I don't have to like it. (If I lost you there, let me clarify: People who like pistachio ice cream are cheaters because I can find no other explanation for why you would willingly take something so good and ruin it.)

As I call down the Métro corridor to my son—"Leo, slow down!"—and wipe drool from my sleeping daughter's chin, I consider I must not be the ad's intended audience. I have neither the desire nor the time for infidelity.

That is, unless Ryan Gosling sets up a profile.

La Vie en Rose

MARIE VAREILLE

Christmas passed with hardly a trace: In the neighborhood of Belleville, neither the owners of the Chinese supermarkets nor the prostitutes on boulevard de la Villette put up trees in their windows. Between the Peking ducks hanging in the restaurants, no one hung up Christmas ornaments. All the better. As of tomorrow, I would officially be a widow for longer than I had been married. I'd have to buy a small bottle of champagne to celebrate.

In my previous life, when I was married, I would have told you that from the dormer of my studio under the rafters, I saw the Sacré-Cœur and Notre-Dame and that the snow, like a coat, wrapped the most beautiful city in the world.

I wouldn't have lied. That's really what I would have seen. I used to wear rose-colored glasses that masked the ugliness of the rest of the world. Everything was to be marveled at, everything was magnificent and beautiful.

Not any more. David took the rose-colored glasses when he left. Now, I see life the way it is. I see the truth, and the truth is ugly. The truth is that my window is poorly insulated and the view is of a gray cement building across the way, laundry on rusty lines and melting snow in pots of dead flowers. That's the real Paris—not the Paris of postcards and American films. It's the gray Paris that doesn't interest anyone. The truth, also, is that I have more and more difficulty remembering David's face.

It's good the rose-colored glasses are gone. Now, I live in reality. And reality is gray. I'm 26 years old, and I've been a widow for two years. It's my fault, of course. Instead of getting married at an early age, I should have done as everyone else does: screw around with every guy in Paris age 20 to 35, then settle down later with a nice Parisian, met on Tinder. Without the rose-colored glasses, that's likely what I would have done.

With this snow, I would love to cancel my evening out with Samantha and her new friends. But if I back out one more time, she'll worry, call my mother and create unnecessary drama. Everyone will re-enter "intervention" mode and tell me to "consult." I saw a therapist for one year. The result (in my unexpert opinion): Me: 1. Depression: 0.

It's true that I still have difficulty breathing when I walk in front of a park and see a couple sitting on a bench. We never went on vacation during August. David worked in a souvenir shop, and summer was his busiest season. I met up with him for lunch, we would buy crappy sandwiches at an overpriced café along the rue de Rivoli. We would sit on the green, metallic chairs surrounding the fountain in the Jardin des Tuileries. We would watch the children play with paper boats in the water. We would talk about our future, potential baby names and buying an apartment. That's where we met, where he asked me to marry him and where I said "yes."

Today, I often make detours of several kilometers just to avoid that green and gold gate. I haven't been near it since the accident. I'll never go back. I don't think I could stand seeing the Jardin des Tuileries without the rose-colored glasses. It would be too painful. I guess I'm not doing that well after all.

I force myself to get dressed. I apply a thick layer of concealer to hide the dark circles, and a coat of mascara. This outing, if I behave somewhat normally, will earn me two or maybe even three weeks of peace.

In the bar, Samantha signals to me. They are a group of four women sitting at a wooden table. They had ordered a bottle of wine. They're Samantha's colleagues, and I've met them many times. I never remember their first names, and they always remember mine. I call them the "four graces," and yes, my tongue is planted firmly in my cheek when I say it.

Samantha made new friends since David passed away. I don't blame her for that. Before, I was funny and enthusiastic. Today, for me, picking up the telephone requires about the same amount of energy as an international move.

I sit down, say "hello" and even attempt a smile. They flatter me on everything: my makeup, my clothing. They pour me a drink and give me the best seat. Being a widow at my age carries a certain number of inconveniences, such as attracting the adoration and pity of everyone on the planet.

I got a raise when I returned to work after my hospitalization even though I hadn't worked in three months. It's because David died. The gifts my parents shower me with? They are because David died. Everyone invites me to parties, on weekend trips and on vacation even though I'm about as fun as a Benedictine nun in a coma… because David died. Everyone speaks to me softly, as if to a sick child. I can say the most idiotic things, and everyone always agrees with me. Because David died.

I haven't gotten used to the furtive glances, sad looks

and uncomfortable silence. Even if I wanted to forget, I couldn't. In reality, no one wants to be alone with me. It's too depressing, and I just might be contagious. It's not fair. I should behave normally with others, yet others never behave normally with me.

Their forced attentiveness chokes me. I smile politely and use the excuse of buying a bottle of wine to get up. The one on the table is still half full. Everyone speaks up. Each friend wants to go to the bar so I can stay seated. And do I need money to pay? I make my way to the bar without answering them.

I want Samantha to go back to normal, like she was before when she would make fun of my hair, yell at me when I was late or talk to me about her latest romantic evenings. I want my mother to lift her eyes to the ceiling when I lean my elbows on the table and to scold me without reason. I want, even for a few hours, to no longer be a widow.

"A bottle of Brouilly," I say to the young man behind the bar.

"I was ahead of you," a guy behind me says.

I turn around and see a tall, dark-haired man with a rather aloof look claim his spot. I don't think he truly was there before me, but I'm not in any hurry to return to the four graces.

"I'm sorry, go ahead."

"Four pints of Heineken," he says.

He could have thanked me. He stares at me without smiling and says, "Can I buy you a drink?"

"No, thank you."

He raises an eyebrow, and behind him, the bartender prepares the beers.

"It looks like you're single, and I asked if you'd like a drink—I didn't propose marriage."

I show him my wedding band.

"Do I look single to you?"

"You look a bit young to be a married woman."

"I'm not a married woman," I say curtly. "I'm a widow. My husband died in a car accident two years ago."

I expect to see his face fall, or him become uncomfortable and say he has to go—and then return to his friends and tell them what just happened. Instead, he cocks his head and looks at me attentively once again.

"My wife took off with my brother, leaving a note on the kitchen table, a week after we decided to have a baby. I think I've got you beat."

I ask myself if I heard him right. I'm close to wanting to strangle him.

"You are ridiculous! It's worse to…"

I stop myself and shake my head. I'm not going to get into an argument about who has suffered more. I turn my back to him and signal the waiter. He had forgotten about me and is clearing empty glasses at the edge of the counter.

"Can I have my Brouilly now?"

"I'll be right there, *Mademoiselle*."

"*Madame*." The man behind me corrects him.

I toss him a furious look. His lips turn up in a slight smile.

"That said, one day, I decided I was no longer divorced," he continues, as if we had started a conversation. "I decided I was simply single. You should do the same. One shouldn't be a widow for more than a year. At that point, you should start at zero. You're no longer a widow, and normal life can continue."

"You find yourself funny? Leave me alone."

Frenetically, I signal the bartender, who ignores me and instead takes care of a blonde who is much prettier than I am.

"I'm not saying that to get a laugh," he says, shrugging. "You don't intend to remain a widow your whole life, do you?"

As if I had a choice. I opt to ignore him and keep my back turned. I never should have let him get ahead of me.

"Seriously," he continues, undaunted. "How long were you with your husband? Considering your age, I would say five years or maximum six. They say it takes about half the time spent together to recover from a breakup so you're almost there."

"This has nothing to do with a breakup!" I shout. "My husband died."

"What makes that more difficult than a breakup after six years together?"

"Because… but you're… I don't want to…"

I'm boiling with rage. I want to scream at him, but I have tears in my eyes.

"I'm sorry," the man murmurs when he notices. "I wanted to distract you a bit, not make you cry."

Finally, he seems uncomfortable. He holds out a napkin. I tear it from his hands and noisily blow my nose.

"Eighteen euros for the Brouilly," the bartender says, setting the bottle in front of me.

"I'll get that, to make up for things," the stranger says, sliding his credit card across the counter before I can reach my wallet.

"Thanks," I whisper.

"I'm sorry," he repeats.

I shrug my shoulders. No one speaks with me about David or the accident any more. The subject is taboo. He, at least, doesn't speak with me like I'm sick or weird—as if merely talking about the accident could kill me. He takes his four pints, two handles in each hand, and, with a sad smile, wishes me a good evening as he walks off.

"OK for the drink," I say all of a sudden.

The words had come out before I could stop them. He turns, looking surprised but happy at the same time.

"I'll drop these off and be right back."

I nod. I grab the bottle and bring it back to the table. Before anyone has time to speak to me, I say, "I'm going to have a drink with a guy at the bar."

"Super!" Samantha says. "The dark-haired one you were talking to? Not bad..."

She checks out the stranger and his friends across the room. Soon the others do the same and start commenting all at once.

"Nice smile."

"Too thin for me."

"I go more for blonds."

"Just my type. If it doesn't work out for you, give him my number."

And then, suddenly, they seem to remember to whom they're speaking, and they surround me with their attentions. Is everything going to be OK? Can I signal them if there's a problem? I don't have to do anything I don't want to...

Samantha sharply interrupts: "That's enough. She's a big girl. She can have a drink with a man in a bar without someone holding her hand."

She smiles at me, and I want to hug her.

I return to the bar, where the stranger is waiting for me.

"I hope your young widow-in-distress protection committee has approved of me," he says.

"The verdict is you should buy me a drink and not crack any stupid jokes."

"What would you like? My treat."

"A glass of champagne," I say as if challenging him.

He smiles, clearly amused.

"Luxurious tastes! I would have done better to pick up one of your friends."

He orders my champagne. He already has a beer. We discuss work a bit, nothing very exciting. Because he is very direct with me, I dare to ask about his wife and the breakup. He replies with the same indifference he might have if he were giving me a cake recipe. I ask myself if he, too, sees the world in gray and if he'll see the world that way for the rest of his life.

"You don't have a monopoly on heartbreak," he concludes. "And I assure you. We can recover from anything."

He seems to have gotten over it. I think of Samantha, who broke up last year with Marc after four years together. She was unhappy. I never spoke with her about it. She tried, I think, to call me, but my suffering seemed profound and hers almost superficial. Everyone gets dumped. Not everyone, however, loses a husband in a Vélib' bicycle accident because of a drunken asshole driving at 80 kilometers an hour on the boulevard de Sébastopol. I might not have a monopoly on heartbreak, but I do have the credit for violent death.

He asks me questions. I don't know why, but maybe because I don't know him, I reply. I tell him about my meeting with David on the green chairs of the Jardin des Tuileries, the walks hand-in-hand in the sunshine, vacations in Brittany, our rare arguments, my burned *pot-au-feu* dinners, sleeping late under the rafters, our wedding in Arcachon, our parents who think we're too young, the names of the children we'll never have, the call at 11:37 p.m., the hospital, the end, and then, since, the gray filter, the life of blandness, the world that will be forever ugly.

He listens closely, sipping beer from time to time. When I'm done, he simply says, "It's true. It is a tragedy."

I continue. I can't stop myself. For the first time, I speak of memories I had pushed out of my mind for months because they were too painful. The words flow on their own, trip over each other to escape as if they've been imprisoned too long. I don't know him. I tell him everything. And as I speak, a soft feeling of nostalgia overcomes me, replacing the heavy weight I've been carrying within. I feel light. I've never felt so light before. Or maybe, it's the champagne.

"I'd like to go somewhere," I say all of a sudden.

"Where?" he asks, surprised.

I drink the rest of my champagne in one straight shot.

"Finish your drink and let's go."

Intrigued, he obeys, and we make our way to the exit. On the way, I signal to Samantha, who gives me the thumbs up sign and laughs. These past two years, maybe I was a great widow, but I was an awful friend.

I tear through the deserted streets and slip a few times on the icy sidewalks.

"It's freezing out here," my companion complains. "We're going to get sick. Do I have the right to know where we're going?"

I don't answer. Even the rue de Rivoli is nearly empty. Only a few taxis dare go out in this slippery snow. We walk past the walls of the Louvre. In the cobblestoned courtyard, snowflakes cover the glass pyramid. I think I'm frozen, but for the first time in two years, I feel almost alive.

Then the dark gate appears, stretching along this silent path to the place de la Concorde. The golden pointed tips reflect the light of the gas lamps.

I stop, grip the wet metal and press my face between two bars. The sandy walkways are covered by a white layer, glistening in the dark of night. It looks as if someone sprinkled the naked tree branches with powdered sugar. The green chairs, covered in white, circle the fountains. Everything is asleep under a thin layer of transparent ice. This white carpet dulls every sound. We can't hear cars or passersby—only the man from the bar, the Jardin des Tuileries and me.

For several minutes, I feel David's presence next to me. Not the David I saw for the last time, in a coma, swollen and attached to tubes that kept him between life and death. No, this was my David from the beginning, with sparkling eyes and a little wrinkle at the corner of his lips that gave me the feeling he could break into laugher at any minute.

I never saw anything so beautiful. Without leaving this snowy place, I ask, "What's your name?"

"Jonathan. And you?"

"Julie."

Then, he takes my frozen hand away from the bar.

La Vie en Rose

MARIE VAREILLE

Noël est passé sans laisser de traces : à Belleville, ni les propriétaires des supermarchés chinois, ni les prostituées du boulevard de La Villette n'installent de sapin aux fenêtres. Entre les canards laqués qui pendouillent dans les vitrines des restaurants, personne ne suspend de boules de Noël. Tant mieux. À partir de demain, j'aurais officiellement été veuve plus longtemps que je n'aurais été mariée. Il faudra que j'achète une mini-bouteille de champagne au chinois en bas pour fêter ça.

Dans ma vie d'avant, quand j'étais mariée, je vous aurais raconté que de la fenêtre de mon studio sous les combles, je voyais le Sacré-Cœur et Notre-Dame et que la neige recouvrait d'un blanc manteau la plus belle ville du monde. Je n'aurais pas menti, c'est réellement ce que je voyais. Avant, je portais sur les yeux un filtre rose bonbon, qui dissimulait la laideur du monde. Tout était matière à s'extasier, tout était magnifique, enthousiasmant, esthétique. Plus maintenant. David est parti en emportant le filtre avec lui. Maintenant, je vois la vie telle qu'elle est, je vois la vérité, et la vérité est moche. La vérité, c'est que de ma fenêtre mal isolée, on ne voit que l'immeuble d'en face en béton gris, les étendoirs à linge rouillés qui pendent nus aux fenêtres closes, et la neige qui fond en boue grisâtre dans des bacs à fleurs, qui n'ont pas vu un géranium depuis l'invention du moteur à explosion. Voilà le vrai Paris, pas le Paris des cartes postales et des films américains, le Paris gris, qui n'intéresse personne. La vérité, aussi, c'est que j'ai de plus en plus de mal à me souvenir du visage de David.

C'est une bonne chose que le filtre ait disparu. Maintenant, je vis dans la réalité. La réalité est grise. J'ai vingt-six ans et je suis veuve depuis deux ans. C'est de ma faute, évidemment. Plutôt que de me marier à cet âge indécent, j'aurais dû faire comme tout le monde, me taper tout Paris de vingt à trente-cinq ans, et me caser plus tard avec un Parisien sympathique, rencontré sur Tinder. C'est sans doute ce que j'aurais fait, sans le filtre rose bonbon.

Avec cette neige, je voudrais avoir le droit d'annuler ma soirée avec Samantha et ses nouvelles copines. Mais si j'annule une fois de plus, elle s'inquiétera, elle appellera ma mère, ça fera un drame. Tout le monde rentrera en mode « intervention » et me demandera de retourner « voir quelqu'un ». J'ai fait un an de thérapie. Résultats des courses : Moi : 1 - Dépression : 0.

C'est vrai que j'ai encore du mal à respirer quand je passe devant un parc et que j'aperçois un couple, assis sur un banc. On ne partait jamais en vacances au mois d'août. David travaillait dans une boutique de souvenirs et l'été était sa période la plus chargée. Je le rejoignais à l'heure du déjeuner, on achetait un mauvais sandwich dans un des cafés hors de prix des arcades de la rue de Rivoli. On déjeunait sur les chaises métalliques vertes, disposées autour du bassin du Jardin des Tuileries. On regardait les enfants pousser des bateaux en papier sur l'eau ensoleillée, on parlait futur, prénoms de bébés, achat d'appartement. C'est là qu'on s'est rencontrés, là qu'il m'a demandée en mariage, là que j'ai dit oui.

Aujourd'hui, il m'arrive de faire des détours de plusieurs kilomètres, pour éviter la grille verte et dorée. Je n'y ai plus remis les pieds depuis l'accident, je n'y remettrai plus jamais les pieds. Je ne supporterais pas de revoir le Jardin des Tuileries sans le filtre rose, ce serait trop douloureux. Je ne vais peut-être pas si bien que ça finalement. Je me force à m'habiller, je m'applique une bonne couche d'anti-cernes et de mascara. Cette sortie, si j'arrive à me comporter de manière à peu près normale, me permettra de gagner au moins deux, voire trois semaines de répit.

Dans le bar, Samantha me fait des grands signes. Elles sont quatre filles à être assises à une table en bois. Elles ont commandé une bouteille de vin. Ce sont les collègues de Samantha, je les ai déjà rencontrées à diverses reprises. Je ne me souviens jamais de leurs prénoms et elles se souviennent toutes du mien. Je les ai surnommées les quatre grâces, et oui, c'est ironique. Samantha s'est fait de nouvelles copines, depuis que David est parti. Je ne lui en veux pas. Avant j'étais drôle, enthousiaste, présente, aujourd'hui, décrocher le téléphone me demande l'équivalent en énergie d'un déménagement à l'international. Je m'assois, je dis bonjour, je tente même un sourire. On me complimente sur tout, mon maquillage, mes habits, on me sert un verre, on me laisse la meilleure place. Être veuve à mon âge comporte un certain nombre d'inconvénients accablants, dont notamment celui de bénéficier de tout l'amour et de la commisération de la planète.

Si j'ai eu une augmentation quand je suis rentrée de mon hospitalisation, alors que je n'avais pas travaillé depuis trois mois, c'est parce que David est mort, les cadeaux dont mes parents me couvrent, c'est parce que David est mort, si on m'invite à toutes les soirées, week-ends et vacances, alors que je suis à peu près aussi fun qu'une sœur Bénédictine dans le coma, c'est parce que

David est mort. On me parle doucement, comme à une enfant malade, je peux sortir les pires idioties, tout le monde est toujours d'accord avec moi. Parce que David est mort. Je ne me suis pas habituée, aux coups de coudes, aux coups d'œil, aux regards désolés aux silences gênés. Même si je voulais oublier, je ne pourrais pas. En réalité, personne n'a envie de rester seul avec moi, c'est trop déprimant et je pourrais bien être contagieuse. C'est injuste, je dois me comporter normalement avec les autres, mais les autres ne se comportent jamais normalement avec moi.

Leur sollicitude forcée m'étouffe, je souris poliment et me lève, sous prétexte d'aller acheter une bouteille de vin. Celle sur la table est encore à moitié pleine. Tout le monde s'exclame, elles vont y aller à ma place, je peux rester assise, est-ce que j'ai besoin d'argent pour payer ? Je me fraye un passage jusqu'au bar sans leur répondre. Je voudrais que Samantha redevienne normale, comme avant, qu'elle se moque de ma coiffure, qu'elle m'engueule quand je suis en retard, qu'elle me parle de ses soirées romantiques. Je voudrais que ma mère lève les yeux au ciel, quand je mets mes coudes sur la table, qu'elle me fasse des reproches injustifiés. Je voudrais, pour quelques heures seulement, ne plus être veuve.

— Une bouteille de Brouilly, dis-je au jeune homme derrière le bar.

— J'étais là avant, dit un type derrière moi.

Je me retourne, un homme brun assez grand, l'air taciturne vient de revendiquer sa place. Je ne crois pas qu'il était réellement là avant moi, mais je ne suis pas pressée de retrouver les quatre grâces.

— Je suis désolée, allez-y.

— Quatre pintes d'Heineken, commande-t-il.

Il aurait pu me remercier. Il me dévisage sans sourire et me dit :

— Je vous offre un verre ?

— Non, merci.

Il hausse un sourcil, derrière lui le barman s'active à la tireuse pour sortir ses quatre bières.

— Vous avez l'air célibataire, c'est un verre, pas une demande en mariage.

Je lui montre l'alliance à ma main gauche.

— Tu trouves que j'ai l'air célibataire ?

— Ah, on se tutoie ? Au temps pour moi, tu semblais un peu jeune pour être une femme mariée.

— Je ne suis pas une femme mariée, je suis veuve, dis-je sèchement, mon mari est mort dans un accident de voiture il y a deux ans.

J'attends de voir son visage se décomposer, qu'il me balbutie d'un air gêné, qu'il faut qu'il y aille, avant de foncer à la table de ses potes pour leur raconter ce qui vient de lui arriver. Mais, il penche un peu la tête et me dévisage à nouveau attentivement.

— Ma femme est partie avec mon frère, en laissant une enveloppe sur la table de la cuisine, une semaine après le jour où nous avions décidé de faire un enfant. Je pense que je vous bats.

Je me demande si j'ai bien entendu, je manque de m'étrangler.

— Vous êtes ridicule ! C'est pire de…

Je m'interromps et hausse les épaules, je ne vais tout de même pas argumenter sur l'intensité de ma peine par rapport à la sienne. Je lui tourne le dos et fais un signe au serveur. Il m'a oubliée et débarrasse des verres vides au bout du comptoir.

— Je peux avoir mon Brouilly, maintenant ?

— J'arrive, Mademoiselle.

— "Madame", corrige l'homme derrière moi.

Je lui jette un regard furieux, il a un petit sourire au coin des lèvres.

— Ceci dit, un jour, j'ai décidé que je n'étais plus divorcé, poursuit-il comme si nous avions entamé une discussion, j'ai décidé que j'étais juste célibataire. Vous devriez faire pareil, le veuvage ne devrait pas durer plus d'un an, ce après quoi, vous repartez à zéro, vous n'êtes plus veuve et la vie peut reprendre.

— Vous vous croyez drôle ? Fichez-moi la paix.

J'agite frénétique la main vers le serveur, qui m'ignore, occupé à servir une blonde, bien plus jolie que moi.

— Je ne dis pas ça pour rire, dit-il avec un haussement d'épaules, vu votre âge, vous n'avez pas l'intention de rester veuve toute votre vie, quand même ?

Comme si j'avais le choix. Je prends le parti de l'ignorer et garde le dos tourné. Je n'aurais jamais dû le laisser passer devant moi.

— Sérieusement, poursuit-il imperturbable, combien de temps êtes-vous restée avec votre mari ? Vu votre âge, je dirais cinq ans, six, grand max, on dit qu'on met la moitié du temps passé en couple à se remettre d'une rupture, vous y êtes presque.

— Ça n'a rien à voir avec une rupture, dis-je furieuse, mon mari est mort.

— En quoi est-ce plus difficile qu'une rupture après six ans de relation ?

— Parce que… mais vous êtes… je ne veux pas…

Je bouillonne de rage, je voudrais lui hurler dessus, mais j'ai les larmes aux yeux.

— Je suis désolée, marmonne l'homme quand il s'en aperçoit, je voulais vous changer les idées, pas vous faire pleurer.

Il arbore enfin un air gêné. Il me tend une serviette en papier. Je lui arrache des mains et me mouche bruyamment.

— Dix-huit euros pour le Brouilly, annonce le serveur en posant enfin la bouteille débouchée devant moi.

— C'est pour moi, pour me rattraper, répond

l'inconnu en posant sa carte bleue sur le comptoir, avant que j'aie le temps de sortir mon portefeuille.

— Merci, marmonne-je.

— Je suis désolé, répète-t-il.

Je hausse les épaules. Personne ne me parle plus jamais ni de David, ni de l'accident. C'est un sujet tabou. Lui, au moins, ne me parle pas comme si j'étais malade ou bizarre, comme si la simple évocation de l'accident pouvait me tuer. Il prend ses quatre pintes, deux hanses dans chaque main, me souhaite une bonne soirée avec petit sourire triste et s'éloigne.

— Ok pour le verre, dis-je soudain.

C'est sorti tout seul. Il s'arrête, se retourne, il a l'air surpris et content à la fois.

— Je dépose les pintes et je reviens dans une minute, alors.

Je hoche la tête. Je saisis la bouteille et la rapporte à la table, avant que qui que ce soit ait le temps de me parler, j'annonce :

— Je vais boire un verre au bar, avec un type qui m'a invitée.

— Génial, le brun à qui tu parlais ? s'exclame Samantha, il a l'air pas mal, je cautionne.

Elle scrute l'inconnu et ses copains à travers la salle, bientôt imitée par les autres filles, qui commencent à commenter toutes en même temps.

— Beau sourire.

— Un peu trop maigre pour moi.

— Je préfère les blonds.

— Tout à fait mon style, si ça ne marche pas, donne-lui mon numéro.

Et puis, soudain, elles semblent se souvenir à qui elles parlent et elles m'entourent de nouveau de leur prévenance. Ça va aller ? Je leur fais signe si j'ai un problème ? Je ne suis obligée de rien... Samantha interrompt sèchement ces réflexions inquiètes :

— C'est bon, c'est une grande fille, elle peut boire un verre avec un mec dans un bar, sans qu'on lui tienne la main.

Elle me sourit et j'ai subitement envie de la prendre dans mes bras.

Je retourne au bar, où l'inconnu m'attend.

— J'espère avoir été validé par votre comité de protection des jeunes veuves en détresse, dit-il.

— Aux dernières nouvelles, vous deviez m'offrir un verre et non faire des blagues stupides…

— Choisissez, je vous invite.

— Je vais prendre une coupe de champagne, déclare-je d'un air de défi.

Il a un sourire amusé.

— Vous avez des goûts de luxe, j'aurais mieux fait de draguer votre copine.

Il commande mon champagne, lui avait déjà sa bière. On discute un peu boulot, rien de bien passionnant. Puisqu'il est si direct avec moi, j'ose l'interroger sur sa femme, leur rupture. Il répond avec le même détachement que s'il m'énonçait la recette du quatre-quarts. Je me demande si lui aussi, voit la vie en gris, s'il la verra en gris jusqu'à la fin de sa vie.

— Bref, vous n'avez pas le monopole du chagrin d'amour, conclut-il, et je vous assure, on se remet de tout.

Il a l'air, en effet, de s'en être remis. Je pense à Samantha qui a rompu l'année dernière avec Marc, au bout de quatre ans de relation. Elle était très malheureuse. Je ne lui en ai jamais parlé. Elle a essayé, je crois, de m'appeler, mais ma peine me semblait inconsolable, la sienne dérisoire. Tout le monde se fait larguer, en revanche, tout le monde ne perd pas son mari dans un accident de Vélib', à cause d'un abruti bourré qui roulait à quatre-vingts kilomètres heures sur le boulevard de Sébastopol. Je n'ai peut-être pas le monopole du chagrin d'amour, mais j'ai le privilège de la mort violente. Il me pose des questions. Je ne sais pas pourquoi, sans doute parce que je ne le connais pas, mais je lui raconte. Je lui raconte ma rencontre avec David sur les chaises vertes du Jardin des Tuileries, les balades main dans la main en plein soleil, les vacances en Bretagne, nos disputes tellement rares, mon pot-au-feu brûlé, les grasses mat' sous les combles, notre mariage à Arcachon, nos parents qui pensent que nous sommes trop jeunes, le prénom des enfants que nous n'aurons pas, l'appel à 23h37, l'hôpital, la fin et depuis, le filtre gris, la vie sans goût, le monde moche à tout jamais.

Il écoute avec attention, en buvant une gorgée de bière de temps à autres. Quand je me tais, il dit simplement :

— C'est vrai, c'est une tragédie.

Je continue, je ne peux plus m'arrêter. J'évoque pour la première fois, des souvenirs que je refoule depuis des mois, parce que j'ai peur qu'ils me fassent mal. Les mots coulent tout seuls, ils se bousculent pour sortir, comme s'ils avaient été enfermés trop longtemps. Je ne le connais pas, je lui dis tout. Et au fur et à mesure que je parle, je sens une douce nostalgie m'envahir, elle remplace le poids que je portais en moi depuis des mois et je me sens légère, je ne me suis jamais sentie aussi légère. Ou alors, c'est le champagne.

— Je voudrais aller quelque part, dis-je soudain.

— Où ? Demande mon compagnon surpris.

J'avale ma coupe d'un trait.

— Finissez votre verre, on y va.

Il obéit, intrigué et nous nous dirigeons vers la sortie. Au passage, je fais un signe à Samantha, qui lève les deux pouces en l'air en rigolant. Ces deux dernières années, j'ai peut-être été une super veuve, mais j'ai été une copine vraiment pourrie.

Je marche à toute vitesse dans les rues désertes et

manque de glisser à plusieurs reprises sur les trottoirs gelés.

— On va choper la crève… je n'ai pas le droit de savoir où on va ? râle mon compagnon de route.

Je ne réponds pas. Même la rue de Rivoli est quasiment vide, seuls quelques taxis osent s'aventurer sur la neige glissante. Nous longeons les murs du Louvre. Dans la cour pavée, les flocons recouvrent les pyramides de verre. Je crois que je suis frigorifiée, mais pour la première fois depuis deux ans, je me sens presque vivante.

Puis la grille sombre apparaît, elle s'étire en silence le long de l'allée de réverbères jusqu'à la place de la Concorde. Les pointes dorées reflètent la lueur jaune des lampadaires. Je m'arrête, colle mon visage entre deux barreaux, les mains serrées sur le métal humide. Les allées de sable sont tapissées d'une couche blanche, scintillante dans la nuit bleu marine. On dirait qu'on a saupoudré les branches nues des arbres de sucre glace. Les chaises vertes, recouvertes de blanc, entourent les bassins, endormis sous une fine couche de glace, encore transparente. Tous les sons sont étouffés sous le manteau immaculé. On n'entend ni voitures, ni passants, seulement moi, l'homme du bar, et le Jardin des Tuileries. Pendant quelques instants, je sens la présence de David à côté de moi, pas le David que j'ai vu pour la dernière fois, dans le coma, le visage tuméfié, transpercé par les tubes en plastiques qui le maintenaient entre la vie et la mort, mais mon David des débuts, les yeux pétillants, avec ce petit pli au coin des lèvres, qui donnait l'impression qu'il allait éclater de rire à tout moment.

Je n'ai jamais rien vu d'aussi beau. Sans quitter des yeux le paysage enneigé, je demande :

— Tu t'appelles comment ?

— Jonathan… Et toi ?

— Julie.

Doucement, il détache ma main glacée du barreau et il la prend dans la sienne.

Peut-être

EMILY MONACO

The first time we meet is my first night back in Paris. It's my first night in the 5th *arrondissement* and my first night in the 33-square meters I'll be sharing with Alex, my newish Parisian boyfriend. The old apartment in the 7th with a view of the Eiffel Tower is steeped in too many memories. I had shared it with my ex and then with my best friend Emese. Now the former is in Spain and the latter is back in Seattle. I have no trouble admitting that I miss my friend more.

At my urging, my friend Matt assembles a group of students from our American University. I've never met them before, but get to know them quickly in the way you can when you're 20 and are eating fondue and drinking wine in a touristy restaurant on the pedestrian rue Mouffetard. When we move on to the Moose Canadian pub, wine is replaced by beer and mixed drinks and shots bought by a stranger.

Alex tires of too much "franglais" and heads home. I'm still wide awake, still not sure what time it is. It's a familiar feeling, and I allow myself to marinate in it, slowly sipping beer and telling more about myself than I wanted to people whose names I won't remember.

The moon is following me tonight. I'm on my way home, wine and night and Paris mixing in my bloodstream. I don't know where I am; my sense of direction is muddled. I see the familiar beacon of light revolving from the top of the tower, but that's not my way home. Not anymore. I wander, wander, wander, hoping to stumble upon my new street, when he appears.

"*T'es perdue.*" You're lost. Not a question; it must be obvious.

"*Oui.*" I know I shouldn't talk to strangers, but this man is far more sober than I am. He has kind eyes and a childish grin, though he must be in his 30s. I'm not afraid of him.

We exchange names and pleasantries, and learn that we're walking in the same direction. He offers to walk me home. I'm not sure I like it, but at this point, I'm ready for bed, and I'm more sure to reach it if he shows me where it is than if I continue roaming these streets. They might as well be nameless for all the help the familiar blue signs at every corner are giving me: names I don't recognize in an *arrondissement* I don't yet know. Emese would know, but she's not here, and I don't have her number to call and ask how to get from rue Maubert to an address I can't remember.

He tells me about his job: He's a waiter at one of the restaurants along rue Monge. He points it out, but I don't see it. I can't tell much about him except that with his dark skin and tightly curled hair, he must hail from North Africa, which means very little to me now. I have not yet crossed paths with enough people with an opinion about North Africans to realize that his life is likely wrought with racism. I no longer remember his name, but I don't ask him to repeat it.

I allow myself to be dragged along by the sound of his voice, the sound of his laughter. He laughs at everything I say, and when I stray too far behind, he pulls me forward under the pretense that I'm just so funny, he can't help but use me to keep him standing.

I'm reminded of Nick, a boy I met long ago walking home on the streets of Toronto. He kicked a can along the pavement and whistled on the other side of Bloor Street for two blocks before I got the nerve to call out to him. He walked me home, and we spoke in French. He kissed me goodnight by my mailbox. Strange, now that I think about it, but at the time, it seemed so normal, so fine. *Pourquoi pas?*

But I'm in a different place now. A different time. I don't want a kiss goodnight, just a way home, a way back to the Parisian and the *clic-clac* bed that is now mine—a folding couch that no longer folds, but remains permanently clacked, never to click again.

He leaves me at the gate and reminds me he works in the neighborhood, reminds me of the address of the restaurant, and I forget it as quickly as I did the first time. I nod and leave, certain we'll never meet again. You never meet nighttime wanderers again.

"Emily!"

Months later, it's dark as I walk the now-familiar streets. It's only evening. I'm heading home in time to make dinner, but in the winter, evening looks like nighttime in Paris.

I turn and see that it's him. What to do, what to do? I never thought he would appear.

"Emily!" He catches up with me. "Remember me?"

Of course I do, but my big city instincts are creeping up on me, and I decide to play possum. I stay silent and continue walking, my eyes on my boots. Go away, go away, I beg silently, though I'm not frightened, just in a hurry.

"Emily! *Mais c'est pas vrai...* You don't remember me?" He's incredulous. I understand. I had been so friendly—the stereotypical American—all smiles that promise something in France. But I don't want to speak to him today. He doesn't understand.

He follows me for a few blocks, chatting idly as if we're friends, as if I'm answering him or even acknowledging that he's there. I don't look up once. Eventually, he gives up and leaves, and I head home.

"Emily! *Mais c'est pas vrai!*" My thoughts echo his words: This can't be possible. I've been talked into buying two kilos of fresh spring peas at the market, and am lugging them home early one Tuesday morning in April. It's been months since I saw him last... It seems impossible, but here he is.

I consider ignoring him, but I have a good 15-minute walk ahead of me and no excuses. I smile.

"*Salut, ça va?*"

He doesn't mention our last meeting. Maybe he, like I, had erased it from his mind, pretended it never happened.

We catch up, as if we're friends. As if we know each other. He may remember my name, but I'm drawing a blank on his. I remember seeing it on his ID that first night when he showed it to me to prove his age.

He invites me on a walk that afternoon. I've already told him I have no plans for the day, and my politeness instinct wants me to say, "Okay." Instead, all that comes out is, "*Peut-être.*" Maybe.

I'm reminded of my aging professor back at the university in Cannes, the one with long thinning hair and spectacles perched on the end of a Gallic nose. He showed us an old black-and-white movie and was disappointed when none of us fell head-over-heels for it.

Les Enfants du Paradis. Three men obsessed with one woman, Garence, "*Une vraie parisienne*," Serge had told us. A true Parisian. And then he showed us the scene, the quintessential scene that, according to Serge, made Garence who she was.

Men flirted with her shamelessly on the street, followed her as she walked. Sure, they were in hats and carrying canes, and my version was wearing a black leather jacket and wrapping his arm around my shoulder at each chance, but it was the same, the same when he asked, "*On se fait une petite promenade cet aprèm?*" Shall we take a walk this afternoon? Like the character Frédéric when he asks the simple, "*On va où?*" Where are we going?

And I was Garence when she coyly answers him, as I smiled and said, "*Peut-être.*"

Back at the apartment that has since become home, I had watched the scene again and was struck by the similarities I had forgotten.

"*On va où?*" Frédéric asks Garence. The presumption of the Parisian man who assumes that Garence—who had assumed that I—would want to walk with him and abandon plans for the day.

"*C'est simple…*" she answers, ever-smiling. "*Vous allez de votre côté et moi du mien.*" You go your way, and I'll go mine.

"*Mais c'est peut-être le même?*" Frédéric says hopefully. Maybe it's the same?

"*Non,*" she answers. In the flirting game as it's played in Paris, women always hold the upper hand.

"*Pourquoi?*" Frédéric asks, pouting. Pouting like that guy had pouted when I turned down his invitation for an afternoon stroll, a cup of coffee.

They spar in the game known as *la drague*, flirting the way everyone does here. People play even when they're married, even when they have no interest, because it's what you do. *C'est comme ça et puis c'est tout.* Neither of us are Parisian, and yet it's contagious. Frédéric wraps his arm around Garence, takes her elbow and tries to lead her in the same way my leather-jacketed man had done the night we met. The physicality of it in no way diminishes Garence's power; Frédéric is the one looking lost, eager, unsure. And then comes the question, that moment when flirtation is no longer just a game.

"*Alors?*" Frédéric asks, like that guy had asked me.

"*Alors au revoir, Frédéric.*"

"*Dites-moi au moins quand je vous reverrai.*" At least tell me when I'll see you again. Please, Emily. Maybe at the Louvre? Would you like to spend the afternoon at the Louvre? It's so pretty in the afternoon. I spend all afternoon outdoors.

As do I, I had answered, suggesting what Garence says next, "*Bientôt, peut-être. Sait-on jamais avec le hasard.*" Soon, maybe. You never know, by chance.

"*Oh… Paris est grand, vous savez.*" Peut-être, peut-être. He laughs at my *peut-être.* I've never met a girl like you before. He laughs and laughs. *Si franche,* so frank. But tell me, when, please. Will you meet me after work?

"*Paris est tout petit pour ceux qui s'aiment, comme nous, d'un si grand amour.*" She mocks him. I hadn't. Maybe I'm not quite Parisian enough for that, not yet. I walk through my gate with one last *au revoir,* one last *peut-être.* I don't know why.

He watches her leave with a child's confusion painted in his eyes. I can still see that guy's face as he pushed it up to the bars of the gate leading into number 36, knowing better than to follow me in, but still begging for a chance, a promise. "Four? Four-thirty??"

Peut-être, peut-être.

In the Red

ADRIA J. CIMINO

My parents named me Jing because in Chinese it means calm and quiet. The name would bestow the qualities upon me, according to the fortune teller who advised my mother. But by some weird twist of fate, the naming of me did the opposite. I was emotional, intense and spoke out when Mama told me I shouldn't. And right now, as I ran through the wet street cursing at the bus pulling away from the curb, I was about as far from the definition of my name as anyone could imagine.

But in my situation, it seemed natural to be more than slightly annoyed. I glanced at my watch, fogged up by the rain, and knew I didn't have a choice if I hoped to get to the bank before it closed. I had to run. I tossed my wind-bent umbrella into the trash can and ran like a maniac along the wide boulevard laden with shops and shoppers.

I bumped into several of my countrymen and women who glared at me strangely, surely not expecting to be run over by a frantic, unkempt Chinese girl in the middle of Paris.

It was clear I wasn't one of them any more. I mean

one of the Chinese. When I went home to visit my parents or ran into Chinese tourists in Paris, they heard me speak French, saw me swap chopsticks for a fork. I was no longer quite the same. But I wasn't French either. I had been living in Paris for four years, yet to my dismay, the Parisians still heard my accent, marveled at the symbols I wrote. Sometimes, I felt like a person without a country. I didn't really belong anywhere.

The sight of that familiar, massive glass door broke me from my thoughts and brought me back to the reality of the soggy weather and the problems with my bank account. For an instant, an image stopped me. Gray sweat suit soaked through, a young woman pushed a curtain of wet, black hair back from her pale face. Yet this disheveled picture didn't make me flinch even as I imagined Mama's horrified reaction. Mama wasn't here after all. And I wasn't aiming to impress anyone. I could be as unquiet and untidy as I wanted.

I pushed the door open. My sneakers squeaked on the scratched-up floor. Luckily, a teller was free and no one was ahead of me because I didn't have a second to lose. I tapped my fingers in annoyance on the counter as the woman hid behind her tortoiseshell eyeglasses and a fan of bills. I cleared my throat noisily, but she didn't seem to hear. I promised myself I would wait one more minute, but just as I counted halfway there, she looked up at me.

"May I help you, *Mademoiselle*?" The glasses magnified her light green eyes into water lilies floating in a moon-shaped face. A look of innocence. But it wouldn't shake me.

"My name is Wen. Jing Wen. And there is a big problem with my account. It's in the red and it shouldn't be. I called the bank three times this week. You were supposed to straighten things out but nothing has been done. And then, today, I get this in the mail!"

I tossed the damp, tattered letter onto the counter. It stated that my account not only was in the red, but I owed the bank money because of it. The woman looked it over in slow silence as my heartbeat quickened. Then her fingers rapidly typed something onto her keyboard, and her eyes narrowed as she studied the computer screen.

"The explanation is simple, Ms. Wen. You made too many withdrawals so you were charged withdrawal fees, which drained your account. There's nothing to straighten out."

"But you shouldn't have charged me the fees! That isn't in the contract!"

"It's the way we operate, Ms. Wen..."

My hands shook as I clung to the counter.

"That isn't what Mr. Laurent told me on the phone!" I was screaming now, and my face felt as hot as fire.

"Maybe you didn't understand... Now please lower your voice."

"I understand your language very well! But I will no longer talk with you. Get someone else for me! Now. I have no money because of your mistakes! I can't even buy something to eat tonight."

"Call Pierre," the woman whispered to an alarmed-looking colleague before asking me to wait a moment.

I stomped toward a leather chair to pout and stew over the situation, but I didn't even have the chance to lower myself into the seat. A man who didn't look much older than me approached, presented himself as Mr. Duval and held out his hand. I was about to scowl and push him away, but the expression in his brown eyes soothed me for some strange reason. Still, I wouldn't let my guard down.

I trudged down the hall to his office and repeated the same words I had pronounced only moments earlier. They were as sharp, desperate and angry as the first time.

And my voice was just as loud. Mr. Duval didn't flinch as he listened to me and checked out my account information on his computer.

"Don't worry, Miss Wen," he said. "I'll settle this for you."

"Like the others? You'll say one thing, and then my bank statement will say another."

He shook his head. "We're going to take care of it right now. Some of the newer accounts have withdrawal fees, but yours was opened prior to that. The funds will be back in your account by the close of business tomorrow. In the meantime…"

He reached into a leather bag, extracted a handful of bills and handed them to me.

"What's this for?"

"Your dinner."

When I first came to Paris, I settled in Chinatown. For a day. Mama had friends there and told me I would be comfortable staying with them. It would feel like home. But it wasn't home. Where there should have been lotus flowers, there were roses. Where there should have been silky parasols bobbing in the sunshine, there were only sturdy umbrellas bobbing in the rain. I couldn't pretend this was China or I would be homesick.

So that is how I ended up in the fifth floor walkup about three blocks from the university. The real Paris. The Paris of students, writers, intellectuals. Even if I didn't truly believe it, I still told myself I would become one of them, that I would fit into this city one day. I told myself that eventually, the woman at the bank wouldn't come out with a line like "maybe you didn't understand."

As I gazed now and again at the passersby stopping for bread at the bakery across the street, my hands steadily wrote out the sum I owed Pierre Duval for the previous night's grocery shopping. After all, he had stood by his word. I was in the black.

I waited for him outside. I didn't want to see any of the others or remember their eyes on me. I figured at closing time, I could catch Pierre Duval alone, as he left. I could have mailed the check, but it seemed like his effort merited a personal thank you. And at least this time, I looked like a human being rather than a drowned rat. As a full-time intern at an investment bank, I had shed my old college attire of jeans and brightly colored T-shirts for pencil skirts and white blouses.

He was laughing, maybe sharing a joke, as he and a colleague exited. His brown hair was disheveled, a reflection of his shirt and tie after hours tucked behind a desk. I took a step forward and was about to call his name, but he had already seen me.

"Is everything OK?"

I nodded and saw relief replace the concern in his eyes. If Pierre Duval knew the Chinese Zodiac, he would say the words my boyfriend Wang said when criticizing my tempestuous behavior: You are too much of a Tiger for your own good. *Or would he?* He was gazing at me with a warm friendliness that washed away any tension of the previous day.

I handed him the check.

"What's this for?"

"For last night's dinner."

He hesitated a moment, glanced down at his toes in a shy sort of way, and then looked up with courage.

"How about if we both use it for tonight's?"

I told myself it was perfectly fine to have dinner with the person who had loaned me money in a moment of need and it didn't represent disloyalty to Wang. (After all, Wang was working in Shanghai and only had sporadic slivers of time for text messages or phone calls. My boyfriend was not dominating my social calendar.)

It didn't matter that Pierre—we were on a first name basis by this point—and I spent two hours talking nonstop over dinner and another two walking along the Seine. I told myself I wasn't the type to swoon because of a bit of male attention and this was about as platonic as platonic could be.

And I told myself the reason I couldn't sleep as I tossed and turned that night was that the stars shining through the skylight were brighter than usual.

Pierre started meeting me after work. The days were getting longer as spring approached summer, and we both enjoyed walking along the Seine and pretending it was still midday rather than early evening. The sun helped us keep up our charade. Pierre was as calm as I was excitable. Together, we were balanced.

He didn't flinch when I told him about Wang. He seemed to accept the limitation of friendship, and I smiled with a sense of relief that I didn't truly feel.

Two weeks passed before the storm known as my mother upset the calm of a warm, sunny afternoon. Barges cruising the Seine cast long shadows upon me as I slouched in my relaxed mode against a willow tree. I didn't see those boats, only felt their presence and heard their sound.

I scolded Mama for interrupting me during the rare break I had from computers, meetings, spreadsheets and four walls. I had exactly 20 minutes. Mama said that gave her plenty of time. She knew I was seeing a young Frenchman. It didn't matter when I told her we were only friends and maybe not even that yet. I could sense her disapproval. Wang was from a good family. The right kind of family. Powerful and respected. I told her my friendships and acquaintances had nothing to do with Wang. I believed my words, but she didn't.

I knew she was shaking her head, pressing her lips together and squinting as I spoke. For my mother, it was clear my rebellious nature would result in a future that wasn't suitable in her eyes. I didn't say anything further. I didn't even bother asking Mama how she found out about Pierre. Mama had a kind of sixth sense, and I didn't question it. She just knew.

Pierre called me three times over the next two days, but I wouldn't answer the phone. I told myself my feelings had nothing to do with my mother. I didn't want to admit she still exerted that kind of power in spite of the 5,000 miles separating us. It went against the loud, rebellious side that was the best part of me. I told myself I simply needed more time alone, to focus on my work.

But how long could I really avoid Pierre? My strategy of scheduling out-of-office meetings at the end of each work day couldn't continue forever. I decided to take the initiative and rely on the courage that drove me to the bank many days ago. I called him.

"I'm sorry," I said. "I'm in Paris to succeed, to focus on my internship..." My words seemed wooden, false.

"It's the way I feel that's pushing you away... I couldn't hide it, Jing."

Tears welled up behind my eyes. I was joyful for what I had discovered and sad for what I now was giving away.

"We're different!" I said. "Will I ever fit in here? I don't know... With Wang, the future is clear."

"And that's all you want?" he whispered. "Something easy? What happened to the feisty spirit that brought you to me?"

Don't waver, Jing! an internal voice commanded. I thought of my parents' struggles, their success and their plans for my future. I could no longer lie to myself. This was about my mother and my father. How could I let them down by not following the path they so carefully laid before me? But then another internal voice—the rebellious one—spoke out: *How can you let yourself down?* I ignored it and closed my eyes.

I shut out the beauty of Paris and the memory of our walks along the Seine. I dressed each day in drabness that would help me melt into the crowd. Like a robot, I walked to the bus stop, arrived early at the office, plunged into my assignments and stayed as late as possible. This monotony continued for weeks.

And then, one day, I woke up earlier than usual. It was my birthday. I would have forgotten if it hadn't been for the e-mail from my parents. Not a word from Wang. I didn't know how to feel. I wasn't sure that I really cared.

What to do in Paris at 6 a.m. when sleep won't return? I showered and slipped into a red sundress for good luck in my 24th year. I leaned out the window and watched the early morning action that I always missed: street cleaners flooding the gutters with water, the baker opening his shutters to shed light on golden croissants, a neighbor hurrying his dog to do some business. There was much to see in this city I had been occupying, yet ignoring, over the past several days.

I would forget about the sadness I had created and take a walk along the banks of the Seine.

A knock at the door surprised me as I was gathering up my handbag and change purse.

Pierre. Holding a bouquet of roses in red that

mirrored my dress. For luck, love, happiness.

"Don't ever fit in," he whispered.

At that moment, I realized my life and my future were my own.

Becoming Parisian

Chaperon et Liberté

LUCIA PAUL

Caroline Dalgrin had one afternoon and evening to herself in Paris. She was determined to make the most of it, in spite of the fact that she smelled like a sweaty athletic sock and probably looked like one too.

Ever an optimist, Caroline had agreed to chaperone the Parisian summer lacrosse tournament for her son Declan's team with characteristic good cheer. She had used words like "delighted," "honored" and "certainly." But now, a few days into the whirlwind tournament with 27 fifteen-year-old boys, she was more focused on words like "exhausting," "hot" and "poorly thought out."

To be fair, it had been the iciest and dreariest Minnesota February day when Caroline first heard about the tournament, and the thought of a European escape sounded dreamy. To sweeten the deal for the six parents attending, each parent would have one afternoon and evening off duty to explore the city (or collapse in the hotel room) at his or her own liberty.

Today was Caroline's turn. But first, she had to briefly darken her adventure with a little mom errand. As she walked down boulevard Haussmann, she hoped

Galeries Lafayette sold compression shorts. More than one of the boys had been entrusted by a naïve mother with his own packing and had arrived in Paris with his lacrosse sticks and helmet, but no socks and underwear. Caroline had agreed to add this task to her otherwise blissful free time.

I wish I knew how to tie a scarf, she thought as she pushed open the doors of the iconic department store. Effortlessly chic women breezed past her wearing classic outfits: a pressed white T-shirt (Caroline was sure they were tailored), dark jeans, flats in black velvet or cognac-colored leather, and a perfectly tied scarf. Oh, the scarf, that scourge of American women and best friend of French *femmes*. Caroline pushed the sleeves of her pale-pink linen blazer a bit higher and tried to look confident.

It must have worked because a saleswoman with a severe chignon and flawlessly made-up face gave her a slight smile. Caroline leaned on the moderately sturdy cane of her Rosetta Stone Level 1 French.

"Yes, *s'il vous plaît, je* search *les chaussures…*" *Dammit, that's shoes.* "*Pardon, les chaussettes.*" The woman led Caroline to an array of neatly displayed formal men's socks. Several more rounds of Rosetta Stone, and the words "lacrosse" and "teen boys" resulted in a handsome man navigating both the language and the problem.

"My boys, they have the lacrosse friend at the fields as well, *non*? This is not the place for these things. Here, I show you."

Caroline carelessly tossed all advice about strangers aside, and gladly followed the man out of Galeries Lafayette and down a few doors to a sporting goods store.

With her purchases tucked away in her new leather tote bag (her husband called it a combination birthday/bon voyage gift), she searched for a café to have a glass of wine. Caroline found a lovely table right on the sidewalk. She marveled, as she had every day since her arrival, that if this café had been in Minneapolis, it would be packed. At least during the four months of warm weather. But in Paris, it was one of countless places that beckoned strollers, shoppers and neighbors to stop for a *café crème* and a croissant in the morning, or a glass of Chablis and salmon *tartare* in the afternoon. Glancing at her watch and the menu, Caroline decided that the latter sounded like the perfect snack. While she waited, she took out her notebook to check her list.

Caroline, like many women, was an inveterate listmaker. She had spent several months before her trip cross-referencing TripAdvisor, Chowhound, Frommer's Paris and the recommendations of friends on what she should do with this precious free time.

Her friend Clara had been adamant. "Darling. You must run to Musée d'Orsay and then sprint to L'Orangerie to see the Monet Water Lilies in that stunning curved room. Then, I would skip the actual Louvre, but *do* go to the Louvre des Antiquaires, which is right across the street. It is the most amazing place… over 200 galleries. And then…"

Asking Clara's advice was like walking into a wind machine. Her opinions and life experience were pretty rarified. She split her time between Minneapolis, Miami and the Irish countryside. Clara's idea of half a day in Paris was very different from Caroline's.

Her friend Nina had offered her own take on a day in Paris. "Pilates is really heating up over there. My instructor trained in Neuilly, which is like the Wayzata of Paris. She said there was an amazing juice bar nearby. Honey, you're going to need some tension release after being with the boys nonstop."

But that wasn't quite the right agenda for Caroline either. *I don't know if I'm really a Paris person*, she thought as she tried to come up with her own itinerary. Her husband had asked, "If you could only do three things in Paris, what would they be? Don't overthink it."

Caroline had surprised herself with the speed of her answer. "Have a glass of wine and a bite to eat at a sidewalk café, browse in a bookstore and maybe buy something impractical for myself."

So that was her plan. Her first glass of crisp white wine had been so delicious, paired with the silky salmon on little toast points, that she had breezily ordered another glass. Not wanting to get sleepy, she had followed up with an espresso and a *crème caramel.*

People were starting to drift home from offices and shops as the afternoon turned to early evening. Determined to find a *librairie,* Caroline paid her bill, gathered her packages and set out to let the bookstore muse lead her. Laughing teens and stylish couples made their way through the streets. Caroline hesitated at a flower shop where roses in muted creams and peonies in vibrant pinks looked artificial but were fresh and fragrant. Deciding against carrying a bouquet around, she turned into the cool shade of a small side street.

As if indeed guided by some internal all-knowing force, she came upon a gem of a shop. *Azure* was casually painted in the namesake color on a wooden plank over the door. Caroline ducked her head as she entered the tiny space.

"*Bonjour, Madame.*" An elfin gentleman was sitting in a velvet chair. Caroline smiled, and he returned to reading the book that was almost as large as he was. A familiar scent of old paper, leather and lemon oil filled the shop. Books reached from floor to ceiling, only some of them on shelves. A precarious pile rested unsecured in the middle of the store. Caroline carefully sidestepped the stack and headed toward the *Enfants* wall.

It didn't take long for that internal guide to offer up the third and final item on Caroline's Parisian wish list: a first edition *Madeline* by Ludwig Bemelmans. The book that her beloved grandmother had read to her over and over. The book that had introduced her to Paris and the idea of nuns in vine-covered houses, little girls in lines, and of course, the smallest girl, Madeline. This wasn't just a book, it was the best of her childhood. It was a beautiful reminder of her loving grandmother and a memento of this special trip to watch her own child play the sport he loved.

With a deep breath, she asked, *"Combien?"* The man wrote a number on an ancient piece of what appeared to be a torn map. Doing a quick calculation, Caroline nodded and pulled out her wallet. As he wrapped her book, she looked out the window at a vine-covered building with wrought iron window grates, just like Madeline's convent. As she took the parcel containing the tangible reminder that she had fallen in love with this famous city years ago, she realized that maybe she had been a Paris person all along.

10 Things I Learned When My Daughter Moved to Paris
ELLE MARIE

I never thought I'd see a bright side when my daughter moved 4,000 miles overseas.

Denver, LA and St. Louis—my kids and I were no strangers to uprooting and resettling throughout their childhood. Because of this early mobility, both of my children have turned out to be adventurous, always seeking out new experiences. Or maybe they were born risk-takers.

My daughter Vicki backpacked across Europe during college with money she had saved from three part-time jobs. I was apprehensive about my teenage daughter traveling to a foreign country with only a friend or two for traveling companions, but I reluctantly let her go. After all, she was technically an adult. What could I say, except, "Be careful! And call every day!"

After Vicki graduated, she worked in St. Louis for a while. She gave it an honest try, but wasn't ready to put down roots until she got some of the wanderlust out of her system. So she took off for Paris.

I shed a few tears but accepted her decision. I expected her stay to be brief, a few months at most. I thought she'd feel lonely since she didn't know anyone there and her French wasn't exactly fluent. The big city lifestyle would be so different from the suburban life she was accustomed to she'd surely be home before long.

Months turned into years. Vicki made Paris her home and not just a temporary stopping-off point. I had to adjust to the reality of being separated by an ocean, half a continent, and seven time zones. Once I learned to accept it, I learned a few things:

1. Paris is the ultimate vacation destination.

Now I had a great reason to travel to Europe—and frequently. The opportunity to visit like a tourist as well as live like a local. I've experienced the beauty of majestic cathedrals while cradling my first grandchild in my arms. I've cruised on the Seine and dined at cozy neighborhood cafés. Paris is a beautiful, magical city—and it's so different from the scenery back home!

2. The French I was taught in high school does me no good.

People don't really say, *"Comment allez-vous?"* (How are you?) They say, *"Ça va?"* (It goes?) Each time I visited, I'd promise myself I would attempt to learn the language, but somehow I only managed to pick up a few phrases, like slang and how to ask directions. *On y va!*

3. Living an ocean away doesn't prevent a close relationship.

Vicki and I talk on the phone nearly every day and email even more often than that. I love waking up to a video she's sent of her kids doing their latest tricks. We FaceTime every weekend and share pictures and news on Facebook. (That's a lot of "Faces"!) Although I don't get to actually be with her very often, I know what's going on in her life.

4. French women really are skinnier.

It's not just an urban myth or a book title. I seldom see overweight people in Paris. And everyone is way more stylish than most Americans. Maybe it's the way they dress in sleek, monotone, dark colors. Or the way they wear scarves. Women, men and children (even babies) wear cleverly draped scarves year-round. It must be a French law. Vicki once lent me one of hers so I wouldn't look like "such a tourist." When I asked what I could knit for my newborn granddaughter, I imagined a blanket or booties, but Vicki suggested I knit her very first scarf.

5. Transportation is efficient.

I love the Parisian Métro, the hustle and bustle of so many people coming and going. Everyone has something important to do, and it's exciting to be a part of it. On my first trip to Paris, I took the train in the wrong direction more often than not and even went the wrong way through the turnstiles several times before I finally got the hang of it. Now that I'm a pro, I effortlessly slip my ticket into the slot, pass through the open doors and casually step into the Métro car.

6. The food is… different.

I won't necessarily say the food is better, but it's certainly different. Whenever I visit a new place, I sample the local cuisine. In France, I've tasted crêpes, *croque-monsieur*, *macarons*, espresso, *pain au chocolat*, and fondue. OK, so maybe I haven't tried anything really exotic like Roquefort or *pâté* or *escargot*, but you don't need to be adventurous to enjoy amazing food. To these Midwestern taste buds, a baguette spread with butter and filled with *jambon* and *fromage* (ham and cheese) is one of the simplest yet most delicious lunches you can enjoy.

On a recent visit, my husband and I took a break from sightseeing, choosing a sunny sidewalk café with a variety of milkshake flavors on the menu. Settling into our prime spot under the awning, we ordered what we thought were chocolate shakes. But when our frosty glasses arrived, they held frothy chocolate milk! Technically the drinks were chocolate, contained milk and had been shaken, but they weren't my idea of a refreshing ice cream treat.

7. Parisians have learned to live in postage stamp-sized spaces.

In college I lived in dinky apartments, some with communal bathrooms. I traveled light and moved often. In Paris, it seems everyone lives like a college student. They don't accumulate many possessions because there's no place to put them. Even hotel rooms are miniscule, though the prices don't reflect that! Café tables are crowded together, and many streets are barely wide enough for two vehicles to pass each other. To make up for it, there are beautiful parks and broad tree-lined avenues. And the Louvre! If you ever start to feel claustrophobic in Paris, a trip around the palace and grounds will remedy that.

8. Always say *bonjour*, *s'il vous plaît* and *merci*.

The French have a reputation for being snooty and unfriendly. I've heard stories of Americans who had trouble booking a hotel room, ordering dinner or getting directions from Parisians. Perhaps it's their approach. Rather than demanding "I need a room for next month," how about asking nicely? "*Bonjour, parlez-vous anglais?* Can you please help me?" I've never had any problems with the French. They're admirably patient with all the clueless tourists invading their city. Good manners go a long way!

9. There's no place like home.

While France is fantastic to visit, I'm always happy to return to my comfortable, roomy home. I know where everything is. All my favorite restaurants and shops are nearby. I speak the language. My friends and family are here (well, most of them). I can sleep in my own bed and eat in my own kitchen. This feeling lasts a few weeks, and then I'm eager to visit Paris again.

10. There's no place like Paris for Vicki.

Though I couldn't ever live in Paris, Vicki's home suits her. She complains about the bureaucracy and cultural differences (enough to fill several books about it!) but it's where she belongs. As her mother, I only want her to be happy. She loves her life there with her handsome French husband and adorable French-American kids. Even though I miss her every day, I'm glad she's in Paris.

(Mis)Adventures at Sacré-Cœur

AMY LYNNE HAYES

We've all got those places. You know, the ones that are the scene of every wild story. Paris, and more specifically the Sacré-Cœur, is the backdrop of many tales from my 20s.

I first visited Paris in the spring of 2008. I was in design school in London, and had popped over on the train for a weekend trip… my ex-boyfriend in tow. Sounds complicated already, *non*? Word to the wise: If you plan to visit the most romantic city in the world, where roses and wine and lights and *amour* fill the air, don't do it with an ex. Especially if said ex has a new girlfriend. Can we say awkward?

Standing on the steps of the Sacré-Cœur, overlooking one of the most beautiful cities in the world, all I could think was, "This is rich. My first time in Paris, and I'm here with someone else's boyfriend. Thank God there's wine."

Still, the undesirable social situation did little to dampen my impression of the city. The sun was shining, *les jardins* were in bloom, and I bumbled my way around town speaking what sounded like half French and half

Spanish (this is what happens when you grow up in south Florida and study Spanish starting in elementary school—it becomes your go-to foreign language). *C'est la vie.*

Fast-forward a year. It was February 2009. And it was freaking cold. I'd finished my studies in London and moved to Paris in the name of additional higher education. At least that's what I told my parents. I enrolled in Paris American Academy in the 5th *arrondissement* and arrived with four months' worth of suitcases—right after a blizzard that rocked the transportation systems of much of northern Europe. I've got a knack for timing.

The winter weather blanketed the city in this damp, white material commonly referred to as "snow." We don't get much of the stuff in Florida. That, in itself, was an experience.

As part of our orientation, the school arranged city tours for us. One of the first spots was, naturally, the Sacré-Cœur. Climbing the steps with light, powdery snowflakes falling is a different adventure. The crisp air knocks the breath out of you by the time you reach the entrance to the Basilica. And there I was again: a new year, a new address in a new country, a new group of people. All part of a new beginning as fresh as the snow falling at our feet.

Little did I know that a semester abroad would turn into nearly three years living in the City of Light. I'd return many times to the Sacré-Cœur, though not as often as one would imagine. When your life centers around the 5th, you find the 18th *arrondissement* to be quite the hike. As in, a saved-for-special-occasions sort of hike.

I next visited the Sacré-Cœur near the end of that semester abroad. Those strangers who'd stood with me on the snowy steps had become close friends, and we wanted to commemorate our time together in a special way. Sunrise at the Sacré-Cœur sounds idyllic, doesn't it? But if Paris teaches you one thing, it's that she teases you with promises of perfection and then leaves you with lessons in flexibility... and the importance of a sense of humor.

It was a Friday morning in May. Two friends and I hauled ourselves out of bed before the crack of dawn, hoping to catch the golden morning light wash over the city. Public transport wouldn't dream of being up and running this early, so we took a taxi. We beat the morning traffic (there being next to none) to Montmartre and raced up the hill.

Evidently, the entire city had decided this would be the ideal spot for an impromptu party the night before. And no one knew how to use a trash bin, or cared to try. Broken bottles littered the steps, bits of baguette and other scraps from last night's picnic gathered in soggy blobs. And the smell... oh, the smell. Coco Chanel and Pierre Guerlain would have cringed in unison.

And the gorgeous sunrise that was meant to bathe the city in light? Yeah, it was hidden behind a building. From every. Single. Angle. So much for that plan. This is where the all-important sense of humor kicks in, because what else could you do but laugh? That and head down to the café at the bottom of the hill for much-needed espresso and croissants. We could watch the morning light bounce off the Basilica quite fine from that perspective, *sans odeur*.

Another year passed, and again, there was a party on the steps of the Sacré-Cœur. Only this time, I was a reveler, singing along with my friends, creating a sizable din. I'm sure the neighbors loved us. The wine-soaked evening lasted into the later hours, and we graced the ears of our fellow partygoers with a chorus of raucous laughter.

What is it about a group of girls having a fabulous time, *sans hommes*, that invites male harassment? Seriously, dudes, we were doing just fine without you. But alas, one decidedly forward young Frenchman thought it appropriate to grace us with his presence… and pestered us until dawn.

His chosen method to worm his way into our hearts? Stealing one of our bottles of wine! *Quelle merde*! Granted, at this point, we probably didn't need that bottle, but it was still infuriating. So we picked up our other bottle of wine—the empty one—and threatened this young man with it until he gave us back what was rightfully ours. We celebrated our victory by washing down said bottle of wine. And paid for our folly ever so dearly the following day.

From tourist to newly arrived student to quasi-comfortable resident to bonafide local, all with the serene Sacré-Cœur keeping watch. There's a magnetic attraction to this corner of Paris: the old bohemian neighborhood, now taken over by a mix of locals, tourists and vendors selling mini Eiffel Towers or woven bracelets. It gives the 18th *arrondissement* a unique flavor. The pinnacle of the experience is a trip up those steps to the top of the hill, and a walk around the beautiful Sacré-Cœur. It's got the best view in Paris.

Just don't try to go at sunrise.

The Best Thing About Living in Paris
LISA WEBB

Everyone kept saying how lucky I was. They couldn't believe I'd actually get to live in Paris. "It's the chance of a lifetime," they told me. So why couldn't I stop crying?

Sure, Paris was beautiful. I'd been there before, and I knew that. But leaving my comfortable, well-established life was a different story!

I'd been married for less than a year when my husband came home from work one day with a funny look on his face and asked, "What do you think about Paris?"

The job offer was too good to pass up, and the voice in my head was already telling me we had to go. But the selfish parts of me were screaming, "NO WAY!" I loved my life the way it was: my family, my friends, my career. I couldn't bear to leave it all behind.

A few months of planning and a lot of goodbyes later, I boarded the plane to Paris. Clenching my husband's arm with my right hand, and pulling a suitcase full of anxiety with my left, I tried to see it as an adventure. But I was having a hard time getting past all the sacrifices I was making.

We spent the first week exploring our new city. There's no denying that Paris is magical. Every corner is a hidden gem, every street impressive. We picnicked, ate, drank and dined. It was the ultimate vacation until reality brought it all to a screeching halt.

My husband had to go to work on Monday—out of town.

I didn't want to be a baby about it. I'd be the strong independent woman he married. I held my head high as I wished him "Bon voyage."

With my husband gone, I sat in our mostly empty apartment and wondered where to begin. I lived in Paris now! But I was unemployed and friendless. What the hell was I going to do with myself? I could only be a tourist for so long. I needed to create a new life in my new city. I decided to start by taking myself out for dinner.

I was nervous. Not only was I going to a restaurant alone for the first time, I was doing it in French. I'd taken a few lessons before we moved, but now, face-to-face with a Parisian waiter, I quickly realized how heavily I'd been relying on my French-speaking husband. Without his flawless language skills to hide behind, I was forced to open my mouth and give it a shot. "*Une table pour un, s'il vous plaît.*"

I ordered a glass of wine and tried to be that confident woman I used to be a few short weeks ago. I summoned her to keep me company, because that chair across the table for two never felt so huge and empty. I was sure everyone else was talking about the foreign girl eating by herself.

This was not me. If anything, I was over-confident in most aspects of my life, perhaps to a fault. But there I was, one person at a table for two, unable to stop the toxic self-commentary about how I'd royally screwed up my life. I had worked hard to get where I was before we moved: I'd built a successful career, made great friends and was never lacking for things to keep me busy. Now I had left that all behind. What had I been thinking?

And that's when it happened. The tipping point. As the waiter stuffily asked for my order, I looked down at the menu. Unable to understand a word and feeling completely overwhelmed with my unraveled life, I started sobbing into my glass of Bordeaux.

That dinner was a long, painful one, and unfortunately not the last of its kind. But I slowly took that sad girl in the restaurant and got her back on track.

If I was going to succeed at a non-tourist life in Paris, I'd need to learn French. I began with group classes, but found it was too easy to become a bystander, so I moved on to one-on-one classes. Those were better, but unless my French teacher was going to be my one and only friend, I needed to meet new people.

That's when "language speed dating" became my Thursday night ritual. Ten euros would get you a glass of wine and a few hours of practicing your French with potential friends. Anglophones were along one side of the table, francophones along the other. We'd start by talking with the native French speaker across the table for 10 minutes. That doesn't seem like a long time until you try it. Then we'd switch, and the French speakers would practice their English with native English speakers.

One evening, I learned I wasn't quite as *Parisienne* as I was hoping to be by now. I was chatting with a friendly Parisian who bluntly pointed out the obvious, as the French always do…

"You're from North America," he said as he greeted me and sat down across the table. When I asked him how he knew I wasn't from the UK or another English-speaking country, he replied, "You're all dressed up like ze Christmas tree." He nodded his head toward the brightly decorated tree in the corner of the room. "You

North American women dress like Christmas trees, highlight your hair and wear lots of makeup and jewelry."

I had a quick look at myself. My highlights and curled hair were my tinsel. Dangly earrings, necklace, bracelet and rings could easily be my decorations. And I had a full face of makeup with lips as red as holly. *Touché, monsieur.* I glanced at the French side of the tables. The women were put together, but understated. Their hair and makeup were natural. Their shoes were flat, and they probably didn't have blisters like I did. A *Parisienne* knows she'll be walking a lot, so she sports stylish, yet practical and versatile shoes. Limping down a cobblestone street isn't exactly fashionable.

Later that night, as my sore feet carried me home, I started to think Parisians may be on to something. Functional fashion was where it's at.

My Thursday night language exchange also introduced me to a woman about my age who had just moved to Paris. Something she said has always stuck in my mind: "The best part of living in Paris is saying you live in Paris." I didn't disagree. When you tell people you live in Paris, their eyes light up, and you're always met with a "wow."

It seemed impressive, but in reality it was hard work. You had to learn a language, walk everywhere you go and carry your groceries up too many flights of stairs. Family is a long and expensive plane ride away, and if you want to call them, you best be working out a schedule to account for the time difference. Friends were difficult to make because many people were transient, passing through or only there for a short time. Nothing was as glamorous as it sounded to an outsider.

Paris was hard to break through, but as the months went on, I found my way. Paris and I eased up on each other. We took the good with the bad and started to bond. I'll never forget going on vacation at Christmas, and as the plane descended, I got that, "Ah, I'm home" feeling that you get when you've been gone for a while. But this time I was landing in Paris. Something somewhere along the way had shifted, and Paris snuck into my heart. It became home.

Paris and I had our moments of difficulty. As I'd pass shops and restaurants where people smoked on the sidewalk, I'd hold my breath, concerned for the health of my newly conceived baby. How dare they expose my unborn child to their second-hand smoke! But eventually quirks like that stopped bothering me, because I stopped noticing them. Instead, I'd enjoy the catchy tunes of the man playing the saxophone in the Métro, grab fresh flowers and carry on, not even realizing that I'd navigated through two line changes. I went from being the teary-eyed girl with sore feet to a local with stylish flats, getting stopped by tourists for directions.

I learned to love all things Parisian. The markets, the walking culture, the food, the wine, the picnics, the little old ladies with their dogs in the restaurants. I loved it all. My husband and I would spend lazy Sundays along the Seine and warm up with *vin chaud* on damp winter nights. We morphed into the French way of life, building relationships with the people in our neighborhood shops, and we became quite loyal to our *boulangerie*.

I still live in France, but I'm now a long way from Paris. I miss the pulse of the city, the eye candy of the architecture and the treasure of unknown restaurants scattered on every street. Maybe it has something to do with becoming a mother, or maybe I've taken a bit of Paris with me, but I downplay my Christmas tree look these days. And when I pass a group of French workers on their cigarette break, I no longer hold my breath. Instead I breathe in through my nose and, strangely, enjoy the smell of cigarette smoke. It reminds me of Paris, where I arrived in tears and left in tears, but for different reasons.

And to the girl who said the best part about living in Paris is saying that you live in Paris, I have to tell you: I think you're wrong. The best part about living in Paris is living in Paris.

Métro, Boulot, Dodo:
Commute, Work, Sleep

Driving Me Crazy
JENNIE GOUTET

I wish I'd known getting a driver's license in France would be so hard. If I had, I wouldn't have come.

Or perhaps I would've set up temporary residence in Pennsylvania, one of the many states with a reciprocal driver's license agreement with France. New York, however, is not one of them—and that is of course where I lived.

Had I known, I would have driven with my New York license (permitted for the first year) to familiarize myself with French roads and make getting a license here a lot easier. Heck, I would have gotten an international driving license! It's simple to do in the States, and then I could have transferred it to a French one when I arrived.

I could have done all of this. But I did nothing.

I first realized the need for a license when we lived in Sceaux, which had limited public transportation. I was pregnant, already mom to a toddler and was stuck at home day in, day out. After I gave birth to a baby and the better part of my judgment, I handed over 850 euros to the driving school across the street.

You might ask, "Why bother? You already know how

to drive."

Ah! Because in France, you are required to go through *auto-école* (driving school) to get your license. I started studying for the written exam, which is called simply (and somewhat scarily, as if from a dystopian big brother society) "the Code," and took a few practical lessons.

But I didn't get very far before we moved to La Défense, where I had to sign up for a new driving school. I received a partial reimbursement of my hefty fee, but still had to fork over 1,250 euros to start over at the new school. And this *auto-école* wouldn't let you take driving lessons until you had passed the Code.

So I set myself to studying.

They warned me it entailed 60 hours of studying (to which I quietly snorted to myself). But they were not wrong. You have to answer 40 questions with no more than five wrong answers. The answer can be A, or B, or C, or D. It can also be ABC or BC or AD or BD or ABD, etc.

Are you still with me? If it's ABD and you only put AB, it's wrong.

And there's a picture of the road where, in order to answer the question, you have to examine the image from all sides—the rear view mirror, what's ahead, the side view mirror. Is a policeman behind you? Is the car behind you too close? Does it look like someone might try to pass you? Will that pedestrian cross the street or wait? I got one answer wrong because I didn't know the French word for "boar." I'd never seen a wild pig crossing the streets of Paris, but I suppose the French like to be prepared for all eventualities.

Not to be deterred, I logged as many study hours at the school as I could, always late thanks to morning sickness (or all-day sickness, honestly) with my third child. All the hard work paid off because I passed the

Code on the first try six months later.

I was ready to start the driving.

On a recent vacation, I read a book written by a Dutch priest, *I Was Brainwashed in Peking*. He wrote about his time during the Mao regime when intellectuals and priests, among others, were imprisoned and denied all hope of freedom. The more I read, the more my jaw dropped. I identified with the way his captors had spoken to him. They sounded just like... the driving school.

"Why, you're not even close to being ready for the test! You need at least twenty more hours before I can present you!" my instructor raged.

"But I'm about to give birth, and I need my license before I have my baby," I said pitifully. I returned home in tears.

Determined, I demanded another instructor who presented me at 38 weeks pregnant. But I failed the test.

You see, you can have a stop light in the middle of a street that has no intersection because it's at the exit of a factory. And you can have an examiner directing your attention to farther up the street, indicating where you need to turn left. And you're trying to translate it, and decipher it, which you obviously fail to do without stressing so much that you kick-start an early labor. Isn't the need for multi-tasking supposed to happen *after* the birth? Not surprisingly, I failed the test. I was screwed.

I waited a few months before trying again, this time with yet another new teacher. This guy was so bitter about life, I had to coax him into good humor by reassuring him what a great teacher he was.

Him: "No one ever told you to do that before, did they?"
Me: "No, it's really useful for me to know that."
Him: "That's why my style of teaching is so great. You learn things with me. I don't want to say anything about Cyril, but you won't learn those kinds of things with

him."

Me: "Yes, I'm so lucky (stifle a yawn)."

Thirty lessons later (3,500 euros and counting) and a few weeks before we were set to move house, I convinced him to present me for the license. He said I was not ready (surprise, surprise), but that he would present me because I was leaving.

This time, the examiner was a real charmer. He grunted for me to go, as I trembled with nerves. We pulled into a huge intersection, where I drove like an American instead of a French person.

Question: What's the goal when you enter an intersection?

Answer: To get out of it as quickly and safely as possible so as not to bother the oncoming traffic or those behind you.

But that's *not* how it works in France. You can have a light that allows you to enter a major intersection, but then... you can also come up against another light or stop sign right in the middle. There's no escaping the Intersection of Multiple Lights unless you respect each and every one.

Which left does he mean? He'd told me to turn, but there were three "lefts" on the roundabout. As the car ahead of me started to move, I followed and... ran the stop sign in the middle of the roundabout.

The rest of the exam was a disaster because I already knew I had failed. When I had to stop and open the hood to point out the transmission (oh yes—you have to know the body of the car inside and out in order to answer two randomly-chosen questions), I couldn't even open the darn hood I was shaking so much. He made a snide comment about what a loser I was.

Bon. I put all that behind me to enter the joys of stay-at-home mommyhood for the next year and a half. But soon it was time to think about that license again. I only had six more months before my Code expired and I would have to start from scratch—including the written part—if I didn't get it *now*.

The closest school rejected me. "You already failed the test. We can't take you. The city only allows us a certain number of spots to present our students for the test, and we give priority to students who have been with us since the beginning."

I called four more schools in the area. Same thing.

I went to bed early that night, "on strike." My husband was concerned I'd carry out my threat to move back to the States where people are civilized. I decided on a fresh approach the next morning.

There *was* the possibility of accompanied driving with my husband as long as I paid for 20 lessons with the school first. The reason we had never done this in the past was that you had to drive accompanied for a whole year after the 20 lessons were over, and that just seemed too long.

However, given how long it had ended up taking me already (I'd brought two children into the world during that time, for crying out loud)—why not go for it now? Even if I lost my Code and had to re-take the test, I'd eventually get my license.

I called the first school and asked if that would be an option. Nope, for the same reason she'd told me last time.

"What? I can't have my license *ever*? For the rest of my *life*? I can't take lessons *anywhere* just because I failed the test?"

Finally, I saw a glimpse of humanity behind the French Bureaucratic Robot. She said I could come in to demonstrate my level, but she promised NOTHING.

And, despite the baby-faced instructor saying I drove like an 80-year-old, I did pretty well for not having driven in a year and a half.

They agreed to train me and present me for the license for the third time before my Code expired. For a mere 1,250 euros. But in the end, I got it.

Now, three years down the road, I was finally allowed to remove the Scarlet Letter from my car: the large, red A that tells the world you're an apprentice. It's been three years that I look for stop signs in the middle of a roundabout, turn serenely onto cobblestone streets that look like pedestrian walkways and stop suddenly to allow other people to take their priority from the right. Driving here is starting to feel normal.

Having a French driving license is worth it if you're going to live here permanently. But the road to get there is *long*.

And it can drive you completely crazy.

Oh Canada

MICHAEL ATTARD

An interesting relationship has always existed between Canada and France. The French see Canada as an untamed wilderness where everyone has a backyard looking out on the Rocky Mountains, owns a pet grizzly bear and speaks an eighteenth-century version of their language. Canadians see France in various lights: as a country of class and sophistication, yet a place where people eat snails and frogs, and hate everything English. As a Canadian living in France, I had the opportunity to experience the reality of this odd relationship firsthand.

Immediate impression upon arriving in Paris was that I wasn't in Paris at all. My hotel was located near my new job in Gif-sur-Yvette, a suburb of the city. The long flight from Canada had allowed me ample time to fill my head with iconic images of the French capital: the Eiffel Tower, Arc de Triomphe, the Seine, the Louvre. Instead, farm animals and the hilly landscape of the Saclay plateau greeted me.

Eventually, I found an apartment in the sleepy town of Palaiseau, some 25 kilometers from the center of Paris. It would be another two and a half years before I would say *adieu*. And oh what I learned during that short yet seemingly long time.

I had endured the six years of French required in Ontario schools and hated almost every minute of it. Growing up in a community where Italian or Punjabi were the most common alternatives to English, learning French seemed completely useless.

Fast-forward 16 years, and I was just able to grapple my way through basic conversations. One bizarre thing I learned—assuming my French was correct—is that French people are oddly fascinated by Canada. They talk of the Great White North as being a kind of Promised Land. But the truth is that many of the French don't know what they're talking about when it comes to my native country.

Here's a quick primer to bring these self-proclaimed Canada-lovers into the know:

1. We don't all speak French. You'll find pockets of francophones from New Brunswick to Manitoba, but outside of Québec, they are few and far between.
2. Canada isn't a land of milk and honey. Unless you're aiming to work in the tar sands of northern Alberta (can you say, "rural back-water sausage fest?"), or are into finance and are willing to live in Toronto (the city where fun goes to die), you'll have a hard time finding a job. Most employers won't recognize your education unless it's from an elitist top-tier institution. You may have 5+ years of experience in your native country, but if you don't have "Canadian experience" (one of the most obnoxious and pompous employment requirements I've encountered) then you're automatically disqualified.
3. Canada is much more similar to the US than it is to Europe. Two-week vacations, work-till-you-drop corporate mentality, bland cities and a consumption

culture. Slight variance if you find yourself in Québec.

4. Canadians are polite, but not friendly. The difference is important. Most Canadians find Europeans rude simply because they speak their minds. In Canada, people don't operate like that. They'll be courteous on the surface even if deep down they hate your guts and wish you'd burst into flames on the spot. Forming close, lasting friendships is not easy unless you're still in high school.

5. It's damn cold. Bitterly cold. But you've never seen a more impressive landscape.

On the flip side, being Canadian in France carries certain advantages. Jobs are easier to find, assuming you speak French, possess a technical education and don't mind the lower pay.

But French office life still has its peculiarities. In the morning, you have to go through the ritual of *la bise* with your female colleagues. This involves a motion where you kiss the cheeks of the other person, only you don't kiss the actual cheek—just the air beside it. You do this once for each cheek, so you can do the math for how many kisses are required for a department with a few dozen people. Woe be the unlucky lady who arrives at the office late and has to spend the first 10 minutes of the day going around "bis-ing" everyone in sight. It's a far cry from Canada, where you're expected to greet a lady with a stern professional handshake that would have met with Mother Teresa's approval.

Then there's the hierarchy. For a Republic that prides itself on its rebellious history, the French certainly hold onto a strict social hierarchy. It's as though the boss is just a little closer to the divine than the rest of us. Coming from the right family and going to the "right" schools is surprisingly important.

And let's not forget the national pride the French are so (in)famous for. This sense of cultural heritage is amplified in a place like Paris where the monuments and landmarks telegraph, "We're a big deal." My native Toronto could not be further from this: a socially cold, barren place lacking any sense of itself, and about as exciting as your typical office cubicle. Decades ago, Torontonians decided to spice things up with multiculturalism and inject life into the otherwise puritanical fabric of the city. We now have an urban center composed of various communities largely separated along ethnic lines, each of which barely tolerates each other's existence. Even second-generation Torontonians identify more with their parents' country than with Canada. While many aspects of life in France aren't perfect by a long shot (*les grèves* and the accordion—Satan's air-bags—immediately come to mind), here they are spot on. A common sense of identity makes the difference between a community of citizens taking part in the story of their city and an atomized population of taxpayers and corporate drones doing their nine-to-five jobs to get by.

The expat experience is life-altering in a way that profoundly benefits the brave soul who embarks on it. You can reinvent yourself, far away from the influence of family and friends who otherwise hold you to who you are now, not what you could become. For anyone daring to take the plunge and move abroad, I say go. You might be met with sheep, or you might be met with amazing, welcoming people.

Either way, it will be an experience you won't regret.

French Office Workers vs. Zombies

VICKI LESAGE

If the Zombie Apocalypse ever happens, I hope it magically eludes Paris. Otherwise my coworkers are screwed.

There is a *slight* chance they'd survive. But more likely than not, they'd get bitten and turn into zombies themselves before you could finish saying "apocalypse." In all fairness, it *is* a long word.

Much as I want them to make it out alive (I'm only saying that in case they're reading this), I just don't think they will.

First, these people know how to panic like nobody's business. "Red alert! Red alert! Someone updated the website and put the square products in the rectangle category! Quick! Everyone freak out! Our customers will never understand, we will lose sales, everyone will starve and now my kids can't go to college! Why oh why is this happening to me?"

"Um, if I may interject," I interject, "it was me. I clicked the wrong button, but I'm about to fix…"

"Someone needs to fix this right away!"

"Yes, as I was saying," I say, "I'm about to fix the

problem." My inner nerd refrains from pointing out that technically a square is a rectangle. We've already got enough confusion on our hands.

"If you made the mistake, you clearly won't know how to fix it. Just let me do it. Ugh, this is going to take all day! Oh wait, is it noon already? *A tout à l'heure!*" See ya. Previously panicked colleague takes off for a three-hour lunch.

And that's the second reason these people won't make it. Nothing, and I mean literally nothing—not even zombies munching on their faces—will get in the way of their breaks. They'll stop mid-meeting for a smoke, and they are skilled at stretching a coffee break until lunch. If they could apply such singular focus to tasks that are actually useful, imagine what they could achieve. They could cross items off their to-do lists, climb the corporate ladder and maybe even end world hunger.

Instead, they're destined to be zombie chow as soon as lunch time rolls around. They'll be so insistent on relaxing over a leisurely meal that they won't see members of the undead approaching for their own tasty snack.

Those who don't panic uncontrollably and who make it past noon will likely be taken out by the deadliest of Parisian office vices: debate. French people have never met an argument they didn't engage in, even if you're on their side.

I experienced this bang-your-head-on-the-desk conversation with Josephine, a normally quiet coworker who has an opinion at the most annoying times:

Josephine: "I really don't see why the boss asked us to do this. It's a total waste of time and only applies in a few cases."

Me: "I know! I can't even think of when we would use that."

Josephine: "You can't? I can think of tons of instances when it would be useful."

Me: "But, you just said…"

Josephine: "In fact, I can't believe we're not doing it already. What a shame."

Me: "Then I guess it's good the boss said it's a priority!"

Josephine: "Oh, it's not a priority. We'll only use it a few times a year."

They'll be so busy arguing themselves in circles they won't even realize I've left the conversation and been replaced by a brain-hungry zombie. What's your priority NOW, Josephine?

One aspect of the Zombie Apocalypse that's almost certain is you'll have to kiss your creature comforts goodbye. No more climate-controlled rooms. In fact, you'll be lucky to even have a room—four secure walls will be an extreme luxury. And if you do have the privilege of safe shelter, the clawing and snarling of zombies will provide constant white noise, making it impossible to relax and let your guard down.

The other day, my coworker Gabriel was running his own personal space heater because the building's antiquated radiators weren't emitting enough heat for him. When he finally warmed his cubicle to the perfect temperature, he turned off the heater. The whirring of the device stopped, and a silence fell over the office. Nothing could be heard except Josephine's contented sigh, followed by, "The best part of my day is when you turn that stupid heater off."

Gabriel wouldn't last five minutes outdoors, especially considering Paris is a cool 55 degrees Fahrenheit year-round except for three days in August when it's a sweaty 100-degree inferno. He'd better hope he's on a high floor of a building with a generous stash of canned goods so he can put off experiencing climate without control as long as possible.

And Josephine wouldn't last a second listening to the soundtrack of zombies wanting to eat her brain. I hope she packed noise-cancelling headphones in her Apocalypse Survival Kit.

For the few who have survived up to this point, their curiosity is what's going to get them. The people in my Parisian office have no fear of a closed door. Especially a restroom door.

When I see a closed door in the ladies' room, I assume it's shut for a reason. Like, someone's using it. Maybe not, and maybe I'm waiting like an idiot when there's no one behind it. But considering these people can't even take the time to throw away a used paper towel, I'd be surprised if they closed a bathroom door after they exited. So it's usually safe to assume if the door is closed, the loo is occupied. No need to jiggle the handle and scare the crap out of the person inside (though at least they'd be in the right place for that).

This annoying habit may seem innocuous, but wait until there's a horde of zombies behind that door, fools. In the ZA, it's always better to be safe than sorry. If a door's closed, leave it—and the possible swarm of flesh-eating monsters—be.

But the biggest reason my coworkers wouldn't survive the Zombie Apocalypse is because they're too busy making jokes to notice the world around them.

The other day, someone stole Gabriel's lunch. It was a particularly heinous crime because it was a homemade sandwich, one made with love, yet eaten with reckless abandon. Did the thief think the sandwich was his? Did he say to himself, "Hrm, I don't remember making this sandwich, but I'm sure it's mine?" Or was it more like, "Mmm, yummy sandwich, me hungry, food now, yum, yum, gobble gobble?" Either way, the person was an asshole. I'm not arguing that point.

But instead of working on any number of the tasks on his ginormous to-do list, Gabriel made a parody of our company newsletter, inserting a Menu of the Week, complete with photos of his daily dishes and an invitation to "Get it while it's hot!" It was actually quite clever. But how many dollars (or euros, as it were) flew out the window while he was creating his masterpiece? How many deadlines cruised on by?

And in the Zombie Apocalypse, how many times would he have received a bite in the jugular while making his joke?

That said, I might or might not have written this entire story while at work. So I guess when it comes to trying to be funny instead of concentrating on the important task at hand (wait, there's something more important than being funny?), I'd probably end up as zombie chow myself.

But hey, I've survived three years of working in a French office, so I might be better prepared than I think.

La Dame de la Nuit

LESLIE FLOYD

I was practically in a scene from *A Moveable Feast*. In fact, as I sat at a table on the sidewalk patio of *Les Deux Magots* in the heart of Paris's Latin Quarter, I was a little surprised to see that I wasn't dining with Hemingway. But since I could barely see my two companions over *le grand plateau de fruits de mer,* a girl could imagine.

I sipped my wine and debated what to tackle first. Lobster tail? Shrimp? Mussels? I finally decided on the oysters. There were only six, and I didn't want Jax and Matt to snag them all while I was cracking a crab leg. I grabbed a lemon wedge and squeezed the juice on the muscle of the oyster, still delicately clinging to its shell. I closed my eyes and bit into the succulent meat, savoring the salty shock of refreshment that burst on my tongue before washing it down with another sip of the crisp white wine. I opened my eyes to find Jax and Matt staring at me, mouths agape.

"Leslie?" asked Jax, laughing. "Should we give you a minute alone with the shellfish?"

My boyfriend Roger had introduced me to Jax shortly before I left New York, where I'd been living for three years. I'd come to Paris for a year to attend culinary school at *L'Ecole Supérieure de Cuisine Française*. Jax and his friend Matt, both lifelong Upper East Side Manhattanites, were here for a semester abroad from Columbia Law. Since my culinary program hadn't started yet, they were currently my only friends.

"What?" I asked, raising an eyebrow. "I'm a woman who appreciates the simplicity of quality food."

"But maybe you could keep the moaning to a minimum. People are staring."

Oops. I hadn't realized I'd become vocal whilst savoring *les fruits de mer*. "If it bothers anyone, they can get earplugs," I said, popping a plump shrimp in my mouth. "I'm studying up for culinary school!" I gathered up my red hair with both hands and twisted it securely behind my neck before diving back into *le plateau*. Jax's phone rang.

"Is that them?" Matt asked. Jax nodded and stepped away from the table. Them who? The fact that Jax or Matt knew anyone else in Paris was news to me. Matt looked at me and winked. "It's his French connection."

French connection? Perhaps he'd found a drug dealer? That wasn't my thing, but I didn't want to be a buzz kill so I gave Matt a questioning look. He continued to grin, lips sealed. When Jax returned to the table I glanced at him. "French connection?"

"I answered an ad on Craigslist," Jax said.

"Oh geez," I groaned. "Please tell me y'all are not making me tag along while you meet some chick who posted a picture of her boobs online."

"No!" Jax protested. "It was in the 'Strictly Platonic' section. Two American girls looking to meet English-speakers to hang out with."

"Strictly platonic, my ass," I said. "Are you sure it wasn't the 'Casual Encounters' section?" He wasn't fooling me. Even if these girls were just looking for new friends, I knew Jax was in it for quite a bit more.

"I swear!" he said, throwing his hands up in protest. "We're meeting them at a pub a few blocks from here. You in?"

"Sure, but don't expect a fivesome from me if things aren't strictly platonic."

We left *Les Deux Magots* and walked up rue Bonaparte toward the Seine. Cobblestones were not meant for high heels. I considered going barefoot, but figured if I chanced it, I was destined to get tetanus from a rusty nail or slip in dog poop. I soldiered on and prayed I wouldn't trip and a rip a hole in the ass of my jeans. When we reached the Seine, I saw the sparkling lights of the Eiffel Tower and smiled. Living in Europe was no big deal to Jax and Matt, but I couldn't believe this was my life now! After a few blocks, we reached The Great Canadian at the corner of rue des Grands-Augustins. And there, smack in the middle of the City of Light was a pub, just like the ones I'd left behind in New York.

The bar was packed, but it wasn't hard to find Lisa and Olivia. Both pretty blondes, Lisa was about five feet ten but had a posture that made her seem even taller. Olivia had bright green eyes and an inviting smile. I knew, without looking, that Jax was already salivating.

"I'm so glad you came!" Lisa said, reaching out and kissing us all on both cheeks, the traditional French *bise*. "This is Olivia," she said, pulling her down from a chair on which she'd been standing and belting out a song by Journey. Olivia moved her Heineken bottle/microphone away from her mouth and gave me a big hug. I already loved her.

I made my way to the bar with Lisa and ordered a Stella Artois, my go-to favorite beer. When we walked back, Jax and Matt were lost in the crowd. Olivia came over from the makeshift dance floor and clinked my bottle with hers screaming, "STELLLAAAHH!!!" à la *A*

Streetcar Named Desire.

Lisa and Olivia had been in Paris since the beginning of the summer and had also met on Craigslist. Lisa had deferred her acceptance to Harvard Law School to intern at a Paris law firm,[3] and Olivia had come for a change of pace after losing her boyfriend and job in quick succession. "What brought you to Paris?" Lisa asked me.

"Culinary school," I said. "It starts next week."

"Oh my GOD!" Olivia gushed. "That is SO cool! Were you a chef in the States?"

"No," I told them. "I've just always wanted to go to culinary school in Paris. I thought that I'd go after high school, but my dad said I had to get a 'real' degree first."

"Ugh, parents can be such a pain," said Olivia. "I can't wait for you to cook for us! That's not an option by the way. You *will* cook for us. Lots."

"Of course," I said, excited that I'd made some girlfriends. "Y'all can be my guinea pigs." Jax and Matt came by to say they were heading out, but I stayed with Lisa and Olivia until last call. Strictly platonic had worked out better for me than I'd expected.

I promised to text my new friends the next day, which was technically today, and gave them both the *bise* before I hopped into a cab.

Next week I would be moving into a studio in the 15th *arrondissement*, but for the moment, I was staying with Guillaume, one of Roger's friends, in the ritzy suburb of Neuilly-sur-Seine.

---

[3] Um, who says to Harvard, "Actually, I think I'll wait on it. Don't call me, I'll call you." I mean, I graduated in the top 10 percent of my high school class and scored nearly perfect on my SATs, yet non-Ivy Leagues had deferred *me*. It's possible I was still bitter, but I was also way impressed.

"*A Neuilly, s'il vous plaît,*" I told the cabbie. "*Au coin de la rue Bois de Boulogne et rue Longchamps.*" The location of Guillaume's apartment was one of the first phrases I'd made sure to master.

I sighed happily, leaning my head against the window as we passed the Place de la Concorde, swirling around the Obelisk to the Champs-Elysées. Even though this was the eighth time I'd taken this taxi ride home, it still looked completely surreal. Passing the gilded statues and ritzy shops and speeding toward the Arc de Triomphe, I couldn't believe my luck.

When we made the circle around the Place Charles-de-Gaulle, the cabbie bypassed the street the other cabs I'd been in had taken and headed farther west. Many streets branch from the roundabout, and I didn't yet know which was which, but I felt we were going in the wrong direction.

"*Monsieur?*" I asked. "I'm going to Neuilly, to the corner of Bois de Boulogne and Longchamps."

"*Oui, mademoiselle,*" he replied, sticking his hand up in recognition. I sat back, guessing he preferred a different path to the other cab drivers. He could have been adding a bit to the fare, but I knew that it cost about 18 euros to get to Guillaume's so anything above that was coming from his tip.

Once outside Paris proper, the scenery is not nearly as exciting. But I did my best to pay attention so I could get a better feel for my surroundings. It was stressful to be a woman alone in a foreign city in the middle of the night with a random cabbie, but I relaxed when I remembered the container of Mace in my purse. I slipped my hand inside the Coach clutch, turned the spray nozzle out and placed my finger on the trigger. I'd never graduated from Brownies to Girl Scouts, but I was still always prepared.

The cab driver turned into the Bois de Boulogne, a

huge park on the western edge of Paris's 16th *arrondissement*. Well over twice the size of Central Park, the Bois de Boulogne was a beautiful forest used as a hunting ground by Louis XVI. During the night, however, I'd heard it was the preferred locale for prostitution.

My cab driver turned onto one of the two main boulevards that run through the park, Allée de Longchamp. As we drove farther, there were fewer streetlights, and the park became dark and creepy like an evil forest in a fairy tale. But instead of wicked witches, hookers started to appear. The cabbie slowed and pulled to the side of the road. What the hell was he doing? I pulled the Mace out of my clutch.

"Where do you want me to drop you off?" he asked, waving his hand in a gesture that indicated the length of the boulevard.

Where did I want him to drop me off?! I wanted him to drop me off at Guillaume's where I told him to drop me off, not with a bunch of prostitutes! Then it dawned on me: The cabbie thought *I* was a prostitute, and he was dropping me off at work.

"*Je ne suis pas une… une…*" I sputtered. Madame Lucera had not taught us the French word for "hooker." High school French should really be more practical. And then it came to me. "*Putain!*" I shouted. Not only is it a choice cuss word (kind of like dropping the F-bomb), it also literally means "whore." So there we go. *Je ne suis pas une putain.* I am not a whore. Nor was I dressed like one for that matter. I was dressed like a 25-year-old should be for a night out. While I wouldn't have worn that particular outfit to church, I wouldn't be embarrassed to wear it in front of my grandmother or my father.

"*Je ne suis pas une putain!*" I repeated as I desperately flipped through my *Plan de Paris* to show exactly where I was going. I threw the map over the front seat and jammed my finger at the correct intersection. "I told you. I need to go to Neuilly-sur-Seine at the corner of *rue de Bois de Boulogne* and *rue Longchamps!*" I made sure he saw the can of Mace in my hand. At this point, I was royally pissed off and quite freaked out. I didn't think one of the working girls would knife me or anything, but we were in a wooded area with very few streetlights and illicit activities going on all around us. A couple of the ladies of the night approached the cab. I just hoped they didn't think I was trying to steal their corner.

"Ah," grumbled the cabbie and threw the map back at me. He slammed his foot on the accelerator, and we sped away. I watched from my window as a couple of hookers threw us the *bras d'honneur*, the French equivalent of the finger, in frustration.

Okay, I could *maybe* see how the cabbie got confused. We were in the *Bois de Boulogne* on a street with the word *Longchamps* in it. However, we were most definitely not in Neuilly.

We pulled out of the park, and nothing looked familiar. He could have been taking me to a human trafficking ring for all I knew. I pulled out my cell phone and pretended to dial a number.

"You'll never believe this," I yelled into dead air. "The cab driver thought I was a hooker!" I paused, listening to the imaginary person on the other end of the line. "I know baby, but I'll be home soon," I said, then rattled off the cab driver's name and tag number that was listed on the back of the front passenger seat. I didn't know if the driver understood English, but I figured he'd have at least made out his name and tag number. If he thought someone was waiting up for me and that I'd given this person his identifying information, he'd be far less likely to sell me or my organs, or leave me bleeding on the side of a highway. After what felt like three hours but was probably more like 15 minutes, our surroundings started to look familiar. I could see the industrial skyline of La Défense in the distance, and we passed the Italian restaurant I'd gone to with Guillaume a few nights before. As soon as I saw Guillaume's building, I glanced at the fare meter.

Thirty-four euros. No way. I was not paying this jackass 34 euros after he mistook me for a prostitute.

I leapt from the cab, throwing a 20-euro note through his open window. Ignoring his heated protests, I raced to the door and punched in the code. Feeling a blast of moxie and not a small amount of relief, I slammed the heavy iron door shut. *This* lady of the night had more than paid her dues.

Paris Legacy

Violette

FRÉDÉRIQUE VEYSSET

Thomas called to tell me that Violette had passed away, but my intuition had been one step ahead. I'd had the feeling before even leaving Paris. It was the school vacation period and my parents wanted to see Paloma. I took a few days off so I could accompany her to visit her grandparents. The return trip to Paris was long and sad. I didn't cry even though I so wanted to.

Violette came into our lives 12 years ago. We had just moved to the apartment on rue Servandoni, and she was our neighbor. We quickly became friends. She was already elderly at the time, but still attractive, lively and well put together with a dash of rose-scented perfume.

Our neighboring apartments were on the third floor of a building without an elevator. I got into the habit of doing Violette's shopping along with my own. I had her keys. We stopped by whenever we liked to bring her a bowl of soup or a slice of cake.

Every afternoon, when Paloma got home from school, she did her homework at Violette's place while she waited for us. It was a solid ritual that Paloma continued even as a teenager.

Violette, who loved the French language and beautiful stories, taught Paloma to read at the tender age of four. I hadn't realized this until the preschool teacher stopped me one morning.

"*Madame* Layracque, it would be better if Paloma waited for the other children before learning to read."

"Excuse me?"

"Paloma knows how to read, throwing her completely off schedule compared with her classmates. She must wait for them to catch up."

The teacher clearly separated each word as she spoke and bobbed her head up and down like a chicken.

"It's too early," she continued. "They learn to read at age six and not earlier!"

That evening, I proudly confirmed that Paloma, although not yet ready to devour *Le Monde* newspaper, was easily able to read her children's books.

Violette's studio apartment was small but bright, overlooking the Luxembourg Gardens. The concierge came by every morning to clean and the nurse's aide stopped by to help her bathe. When I picked up Paloma in the evening, we spoke of this and that, or sometimes my job. I treasured these calm moments with her as we sipped sage tea.

When we had first moved into the building, Violette would come with Paloma and me to the gardens, but soon the three flights became too much.

"It's my arthritis!" complained Violette.

Her back was hunched, but curiously, her hands were beautiful. They were always manicured, and rings decorated each finger.

Violette's attorney had taken care of everything. She had received precise instructions for the Mass, the cemetery, the flowers. A few days before the burial, she called us to attend the reading of the will.

"I hope she didn't have any gambling debts,"

Thomas whispered to me.

The attorney overheard him and looked at us with bewilderment over the rim of her glasses.

"*Mademoiselle* Violette Caron, born the first of August, 1917 in Paris."

After that point, I can't remember a thing except that we inherited the apartment on the rue Servandoni and everything inside. An apartment of 1,575 square feet, the attorney specified.

"More than fifteen hundred square feet?" Thomas cut her off. "There must be a mistake. That studio apartment measures about two fifty!"

Annoyed, the attorney repeated, "I leave to *Monsieur* and *Madame* Thomas Layracque apartment number six at 17, rue Servandoni, Paris 75006, which includes 1,575 square feet of space on the third floor, with all the furnishings, jewelry and various objects it contains."

Incredulously, I looked at Thomas.

"Is this a joke? The only other apartment on the floor is ours. And number six is a studio apartment!"

The attorney, continuing her reading, pushed a stack of papers in our direction. On it, in elegant nineteenth-century-style handwriting, was written: Violette Caron, 17, rue Servandoni, Paris 75006. Thomas was motionless and silent. One eyebrow rose slightly, showing his concentration.

"Violette didn't have any family?"

"No. You became her family. She was isolated before your arrival. Other than you, she saw no one and was happy that way. People, in general, exasperated her. Your daughter charmed her, though. She was crazy about that child and the young woman she has become."

We left, sad at the loss of Violette, but happy to have learned we had been so important to her.

"Oh, and I forgot," the attorney said. "You have also inherited the little Renoir."

On our way back to our apartment, we stopped at Violette's studio. Everything remained the same: the rose scent, the blue silk peignoir hung behind the door and the little Renoir that I'd always taken for a good copy of the top of a chocolate box.

I let out a nervous laugh. "It's crazy, isn't it?" I said to Thomas.

He walked around the apartment, examining and softly touching the walls. "If the attorney says it's more than one thousand five hundred square feet then that has to be the case! And it must be on this side because our apartment is on the other side." He took a spoon and started tapping the wall. "Listen! It sounds hollow."

I leaned toward the wall. "Not at all. It sounds the same all around."

"I'm going to get my tools, and we'll see," Thomas said with determination.

"You're not going to demolish the wall, are you? Maybe there's another opening? Let's look in this cabinet. It might be masking a door…"

On the lowest shelf, there were dozens of rolls of toilet paper (enough to wipe the bottoms of the whole building), boxes of tissues, sachets of lavender and a variety of cleaning products. On the middle shelves were towels (enough for an entire hotel), and on the top shelves, colorful, methodically stacked boxes.

It took a few minutes to empty everything, remove the shelves and take down the large wooden panel. Poorly attached in the first place, the wood fell away easily as Thomas pushed his shoulder against it. As I'd suspected, the armoire was there to hide the old door.

I looked for a flashlight in a drawer in the kitchen. I was excited, but scared at the same time. It seemed Thomas was, too, because he didn't dare move forward into the darkness without a source of light. Hand-in-hand, with the illumination of our flashlight, we crept into a hallway covered with flowery wallpaper. The dry, dusty odor was almost suffocating. I bumped into a piece of furniture.

"Damn, we need more light," Thomas said. "I hope we're not going to find a mummified cadaver like in *Psycho*!"

He opened a door to a room. The windows were covered with boards. Thankfully, the chairs that held the boards in place were easy to move. Windows and shutters open, sun lit the room like a movie-theater projector.

Everything was still under the ivory dust that danced in the rays of light. The wall was covered in silky wallpaper from pink to pale green. Chairs, a couch, rugs and furniture, all in peach, pink or light green, an open book on a small table and a dried bouquet of flowers seemed to wait for the return of the apartment's owners.

In a curio cabinet, I admired delicate knick-knacks and a blue vase with images of pheasants. I later would learn it was a work of Eugène Collinot.

The three other rooms were just as beautiful and refined as the first. One was particularly astonishing. An imposing bed filled it almost entirely. Heavy, embroidered drapes and wall fabric seemed to protect it from the outside world. The dressing table, filled with brushes, creams and every possible lotion and potion, lacked only a bit of life.

I opened one of the drawers and mechanically searched through it. Under tissues and lace, I found a small notebook. The pages were filled with names and numbers. I read in a low voice without understanding.

"Thomas, come and listen to this!"

November 1907
Monsieur de J., 2 n., 2000
Monsieur de B., Deauville, 6000

P de G., 2 w.: 1 bracelet (Boucheron), 1 diamond ring (Boucheron), 1 brooch, 10 bouquets, dresses by Worth

December 1907
G.D. Serge, 3 w.: 1 necklace Chaumet, rubies and diamonds + rings

February 1907
Monsieur C., 2 n., 2000
Monsieur de H., 3 d., 4000…

All of the pages were filled with the same small, neat handwriting, year after year until 1910. I read her notes but didn't truly comprehend them. Thomas exploded with laughter.

"You discovered her record book!"

Perplexed, I looked at him.

"It's obvious!" he exclaimed, ripping the book from my hands. "Two n. for two nights, w. for week, and so on and so forth. And next to each gentleman's name, the amount that it cost him! Violette's mother was a kept woman… a prostitute, if you prefer!"

My mouth remained half open as Thomas continued.

"A high-class prostitute, but a prostitute all the same! That's why everything is closed up. Violette wanted to hide her mother's scandalous past. Incredible."

In the 12 years we'd known each other, Violette never spoke with me of her mother. She told me about Margaux, her nanny, and the long walks around the Luxembourg Gardens with its puppets and old wooden merry-go-round, her vacations on the Deauville shore. But her mother seemed absent from her life.

"In the next room, there's a portrait of a woman. That must be her… Come have a look!"

A superb creature, with full lips, a fine, straight nose and an engaging gaze. Her figure was perfect, with smooth, milk-white skin. She seemed to say to us in an amused tone, "You didn't expect this, now did you?"

It took us nearly a week to clean and organize everything. I bought trunks at the BHV department store: one for the clothing, another for the letters, notebooks, telegrams, business cards and photos. An appraiser would be coming for the furniture, rugs and paintings. As I moved furniture to better clean the apartment, I discovered several pieces of jewelry. Violette hadn't known all of her mother's hiding places. Hortense—that was her name—kept everything.

Her many lovers, often incredibly rich, had been generous with this woman who we learned was authoritarian and spirited. Hortense took note of everything in a cold and administrative fashion. She even left behind a journal, but I only found part of it. One sentence came back again and again: *Don't end up like Nana*. Contrary to Zola's heroine, who threw her money out the window, Hortense saved and counted like an old *bourgeoise* woman.

She became greedy, and her notebooks were a testament to that. She inspected the kitchen every morning and every evening, forbidding and punishing wastefulness. She would ask the cook to use the leftovers the next day and would save the last drops of wine to make vinegar. Even bread was weighed and counted. They ate meat once a month. Hortense lived in fear of returning to the poverty of her childhood. The days of *not having to put up with men*, as she wrote in her notebook, she ate soup and bread. In 1897, she "tortured" and fired four cooks: *Not clean enough and not frugal enough*, she noted each time in her journal.

As I gathered all of the elements, after several days of reading and sorting through documents, I little by little put together the story of Hortense de Cléry, or Hortense Gibier, to use her real name.

I even seek help from a genealogist, who assists with the research. Hortense, born January 4, 1873, is the daughter of a family of vegetable sellers from Gâtinais. Impoverished, she escapes this misery at age 15 for Paris and for a man. We catch up with her in 1890 in a Montmartre theater. A newspaper clipping Hortense kept in an album mentions her as a terrible actress but a great beauty. In 1895, we find her at the Européen theater in her dressing room. She is surrounded by bankers, grand dukes, Russian princes, the King of Bavaria, the King of Portugal, the Prince of Wales, French political figures… Perhaps she was a pitiful actress, but what a path she traveled in the period of a few years.

The notebook from 1894, when she was only 21, is a long list of numbers and almost a jeweler's catalog, listing the price, description and size of stones offered by her lovers. In some cases, she even noted the weight of the jewels. I discover that Hortense is ambitious. She takes Russian language classes and her first investment with the money she made "lying down" is to learn to read and write. In 1901, she leaves for Russia for a few months and comes back extremely wealthy, forever shielded from the grips of poverty.

Other books—this time hidden in the bathroom—tell me where the money is invested: in the French railroads and apartments. She refuses to have anything to do with Russian borrowers! She prefers to keep a close eye on her investments.

After learning her habits, I'm now used to looking under each piece of wooden flooring or rug, double checking hems, inspecting the nooks and crannies of vases and even pages of her books! It's as if I'm on a treasure hunt. Each object discovered, even if holding no monetary value, fills me with a childlike joy. Obsessed with Hortense, I stop working.

I find no trace of her daughter—either in photos or

notebooks. I ask myself if Violette destroyed everything or if it is her mother's indifference that pushed her to construct a wall separating herself from the memories?

One evening, as I explore a nightstand, I discover a packet of letters hidden under a marble panel. One hundred and seventy-two love letters and three photos of a handsome soldier with a charming mustache. He looks to be about 30.

He is a pilot. They wrote from February 5, 1913 to December 28, 1916. In one of the photos, he poses in front of his airplane. He is younger than Hortense, and I understand that he is Violette's father. Tied with a ribbon, a short letter from a fellow pilot dated January 3, 1917 tells Hortense that Louis Goldstein has died in combat. It is at this date that all of Hortense's notebooks stop, as if counting, stacking and organizing no longer would be important from this moment forward.

Violette

FRÉDÉRIQUE VEYSSET

Thomas m'avait appelée pour m'annoncer la mort de Violette. J'en avais eu le pressentiment au moment de quitter Paris. Mais c'étaient les vacances scolaires et mes parents voulaient voir Paloma. En l'accompagnant, je m'étais octroyé quelques jours de vacances. Mon retour en train sur Paris, fut triste et long. Je ne pleurais pas alors que j'en avais tellement envie.

Violette était entrée dans notre vie douze ans plus tôt. Nous venions d'emménager rue Servandoni, elle était notre voisine et très vite nous étions devenus amis. Elle était déjà âgée, mais toujours jolie, fraîche, souriante et bien coiffée, sentant toujours une eau de toilette à la rose. Nos appartements, voisins, se trouvaient au troisième étage sans ascenseur. J'avais pris l'habitude de faire ses courses avec les miennes. J'avais ses clefs. On passait quand on voulait pour lui déposer une soupe, un gratin ou un gâteau. Tous les après-midis, de retour de l'école, Paloma nous attendait chez elle en faisant ses devoirs : un solide rituel respecté, malgré l'adolescence... Violette, amoureuse de la langue française et des belles histoires, lui avait appris à lire quand elle avait à peine quatre ans.

Je ne m'en étais jamais aperçu jusqu'à ce que sa maîtresse de maternelle, un matin, m'interpelle :

— Madame Layracque, ce serait bien que Paloma attende les autres pour apprendre à lire.

— Comment ça ?

— Oui Paloma sait lire et elle est décalée par rapport à ses camarades de classe. Il faudrait qu'elle les attende.

Elle séparait bien les mots en parlant et hochait de la tête, comme une poule.

— C'est trop tôt, c'est dans deux ans qu'elle pourra apprendre, pas avant !

En effet, le soir j'avais pu vérifier avec fierté que Paloma, sans pour autant être capable de déchiffrer Le Monde, pouvait facilement lire ses livres d'enfants.

Le studio de Violette était petit mais lumineux et il donnait sur le Jardin du Luxembourg. La gardienne montait tous les matins faire le ménage puis l'aide-soignante passait pour la toilette. Quand je récupérais Paloma en fin de journée, on parlait de tout et du petit rien de la vie, de mon travail. J'aimais ces moments calmes avec elle à boire une tisane de sauge. Au début de notre arrivée, Violette venait avec Paloma et moi au Luxembourg, mais très vite les trois étages à descendre puis à remonter étaient devenus trop fatigants.

— C'est mon arthrose ! se plaignait Violette.

Son dos était tout courbé mais curieusement ses mains étaient impeccables, toujours manucurées, les doigts ornés de bagues.

La notaire de Violette s'était occupée de tout, elle avait reçu des instructions très précises pour la messe, le cimetière, les fleurs. Quelques jours après l'enterrement, elle nous avait convoqués pour la lecture du testament.

— J'espère qu'elle n'avait pas de dettes de jeux… m'avait soufflé Thomas.

La notaire l'avait entendu et nous avait regardés par-dessus ses lunettes d'un air consterné.

— Mademoiselle Violette Caron, née le premier août 1917 à Paris.

Je ne me souviens de rien d'autre sauf que nous héritions de l'appartement de la rue Servandoni et de tout son contenu. Appartement de 150 m2 avait précisé la notaire.

— 150 m2 ? Vous devez faire erreur, le studio ne fait que 25 m2 ! avait coupé Thomas.

Irritée la notaire avait répété :

— Je lègue à Monsieur et Madame Thomas Layracque (…) l'appartement lot numéro 6 au 17, rue Servandoni Paris 75006, d'une surface de 150 m2 au troisième étage, avec tous les meubles meublants, bijoux et objets divers qui le garnissent.

Je regardais Thomas, incrédule.

— C'est une blague ? Il n y a pas d'autre appartement que le nôtre à cet étage, le numéro 6 est un studio !

La notaire, tout en poursuivant sa lecture, poussa vers nous un dossier sur lequel, d'une belle écriture de directeur d'école du siècle dernier, était noté : *Violette Caron. 17, rue Servandoni Paris 75006.* Thomas était immobile, silencieux, son sourcil droit remontait légèrement : preuve qu'il était concentré.

— Violette n'avait pas de descendance ?

— Non, et vous étiez devenus sa famille. Elle était très isolée avant votre arrivée. A part vous, elle ne voyait personne et s'en portait très bien. D'ailleurs, les gens l'exaspéraient en général. C'est votre fille qui l'a conquise, elle était folle de cette enfant puis de la jeune fille qu'elle est devenue.

Nous étions repartis, intrigués, tristes de l'absence de Violette mais heureux d'apprendre que nous avions été importants pour elle.

— Ah j'oubliais : vous héritez aussi du petit Renoir.

Bien sûr, en remontant chez nous, nous nous étions arrêtés au studio. Rien n'avait bougé : l'odeur de rose, le peignoir en soie bleu pâle, accroché derrière la porte, et le fameux petit Renoir que j'avais toujours pris pour une très bonne reproduction d'un couvercle de boîte de chocolat. Je me mis à rire nerveusement.

— C'est dingue, non ? dis-je à Thomas.

Thomas faisait le tour du studio, scrutant les murs et les caressants de la main.

— Si la notaire parle de 150 m2, c'est qu'il y a 150 m2 ! Et c'est forcément de ce côté parce que ce mur donne chez nous.

Il prit une cuillère et se mis à donner des petits coups.

— Ecoute : ça sonne creux !

Je me penchai vers le mur.

— Pas du tout, ça sonne pareil partout !

— Je vais chercher mes outils, on verra bien, ajouta Thomas déterminé.

— Tu ne vas pas démolir le mur quand même ? Il y a peut-être une autre ouverture ? Fouillons ce placard, il pourrait dissimuler une porte…

Sur l'étagère du bas, il y avait des dizaines de rouleaux de papier hygiénique, de quoi essuyer les fesses de tout l'immeuble, puis des boîtes de kleenex, des sacs de lavande et des produits d'entretien. Sur les étagères du milieu, du linge de maison, de quoi garnir tout un hôtel et sur celles du haut, des boîtes en carton de couleur, méthodiquement empilées. Cela nous prit plusieurs minutes pour tout vider, ôter les étagères et tomber sur une grosse planche en bois recouverte de peinture blanche. Mal fixée, la planche céda sous les coups d'épaules de Thomas. Comme je le pressentais, l'armoire avait été conçue de façon à dissimuler une ancienne porte.

Je cherchais une lampe de poche dans un tiroir de la table de la cuisine. J'étais excitée mais j'avais un peu peur. Thomas aussi, je crois, car il n'avait pas osé s'aventurer sans lumière dans cette ouverture noire. Main dans la main, éclairés par le rond blanc de la lampe électrique, on avançait dans un couloir, recouvert d'un papier peint à fleurs. L'odeur sèche, de poussière et de renfermé, était suffocante par moment. Je me heurtai à un meuble.

— Merde, il faut faire plus de lumière... râla Thomas. J'espère qu'on ne va trouver un cadavre momifié, comme dans *Psychose* !

Il ouvrit une porte qui donnait sur une pièce dont les fenêtres étaient obstruées par des planches. Heureusement, seuls des fauteuils faciles à déplacer les calaient. Fenêtres et volets ouverts, le soleil comme un projecteur de théâtre éclaira la chambre.

Tout était figé sous une poussière ivoire que l'air frais faisait virevolter dans les rayons de lumière. Le mur était recouvert de tentures en soie à motifs fleuris, dans un dégradé de rose ravissant et de vert passé. Fauteuils, banquette, tapis et meubles, dans des tons de pêche, de rose ou de vert amande, un livre ouvert sur un guéridon, un bouquet complètement desséché semblaient attendre le retour de promenade des propriétaires. Dans une vitrine, j'admirais plusieurs bibelots délicats et un vase bleu à décor de faisans. J'appris plus tard qu'il s'agissait d'un Eugène Collinot.

Les trois autres pièces étaient aussi belles et raffinées que le premier salon, l'une d'elle était particulièrement étonnante. Un lit superbe et imposant la remplissait presque entièrement. De lourds rideaux brodés et les tissus moelleux des murs semblaient la préserver du dehors. La table de toilette, sur laquelle ne manquaient aucune brosse, aucune crème, aucun onguent, n'attendait juste qu'un peu de vie. J'ouvris un des petits tiroirs et commençai à fouiller, machinalement. Sous les mouchoirs en dentelle, je tombai sur un petit carnet. Ses pages étaient remplies de noms et de chiffres. Je lisais à voix basse, sans comprendre.

— Thomas, viens... écoute ça !

Novembre 1907
Monsieur de J., 2 n., 2000
Monsieur de B, Deauville, 6000
P de G, 2 s. : 1 brac (Boucheron), 1 bague diamant (Boucheron),
1 broche, 10 bouquets, robes Worth

Décembre 1907
G.D. Serge, 3 s. 1 collier Chaumet, rubis et diamants + bagues

Février 1907
Monsieur C., 2 n., 2000
Monsieur de H., 3 j., 4000…

Toutes les pages étaient remplies de la même petite écriture sage et alignée, année après année jusqu'en 1910. Je lisais ces notes sans vraiment les comprendre. Thomas éclata de rire.

— Tu as découvert son livre de compte !

Je le regardais, perplexe.

— Mais c'est évident ! s'écria-t-il en m'arrachant le carnet des mains. « *2 n.* pour 2 nuits, *s.* pour semaine, ainsi de suite… Et à chaque fois, à côté du nom du monsieur, ce que ça lui a coûté ! La mère de Violette était une demi-mondaine, une horizontale, une pute quoi si tu préfères !

Je restai bouche bée. Thomas continuait :

— Une pute de luxe, certes, mais une pute tout de même ! C'est pour ça que tout est muré : elle a voulu planquer le passé sulfureux de sa mère ! C'est incroyable…

En douze ans, jamais Violette ne m'avait parlé de sa mère. Elle me racontait Margaux, sa gouvernante, et ses balades au Luxembourg avec le guignol et le manège de chevaux de bois, ses vacances au bord de la mer à Deauville… Mais sa mère semblait comme absente de sa vie.

— Dans l'autre pièce il y a le portrait d'une femme : ça doit être elle... Viens voir !

Une superbe créature, la bouche pulpeuse, nez droit, le regard direct et clair, corps souple, la peau laiteuse et lisse, semblait nous dire, amusée : « Vous ne vous y attendiez pas ? N'est-ce pas ? ».

Il nous fallut presque une semaine pour nettoyer, trier et classer. J'avais acheté des malles au BHV : une pour les vêtements et une autre pour les lettres, carnets, télégrammes, cartes de visites et photos. Un expert devait venir pour le mobilier, les tapis et les tableaux. En déplaçant les meubles pour faire le ménage, j'avais trouvé quelques bijoux. Violette ne semblait pas connaître les cachettes de sa mère. Hortense, c'était son prénom, gardait tout.

Ses nombreux amants, souvent immensément riches, avaient été généreux avec cette femme que nous devinions autoritaire et pleine d'esprit. Hortense avait tout noté, consigné de façon froide et administrative. Elle avait même laissé un journal mais je n'en avais retrouvé qu'une partie. Une phrase revenait souvent : *Ne pas finir comme Nana*. Contrairement à l'héroïne de Zola qui jetait son argent au vent, Hortense économisait et comptait en vraie petite bourgeoise. Elle était même avare, les carnets en témoignaient. Elle inspectait la cuisine tous les matins et tous les soirs, interdisait et punissait le gaspillage, demandant à la cuisinière d'accommoder les restes, gardant les fonds de vin pour en faire du vinaigre. Le pain était pesé, compté. On mangeait de la viande une fois par mois. Hortense vivait dans la terreur de manquer et de retourner à la misère. Les jours *sans avoir à supporter les hommes*, comme elle l'écrivait dans son carnet, elle se nourrissait de soupe et de pain. En 1897, elle avait « torturé » et viré quatre cuisinières : *Pas assez propre ni assez économe* notait-elle chaque fois dans son journal.

En recoupant tous les éléments, après plusieurs jours

de lecture de tout ce fatras de documents, je reconstitue peu à peu l'histoire d'Hortense de Cléry, Hortense Gibier de son vrai nom. Je m'offre même l'aide d'un généalogiste, qui fait des recherches de son côté. Hortense, née le 4 Janvier 1873, est la fille d'une famille de maraîchers du Gâtinais, visiblement très pauvre, elle fuit cette misère à quinze ans, pour Paris et pour un homme. On retrouve sa trace en 1890 dans un théâtre de Montmartre, une coupure de journal, gardée par elle dans un album, la mentionne comme piètre actrice, mais d'une grande beauté. On la retrouve en 1895 au théâtre Européen, dans sa loge, se pressent des banquiers, des Grands Ducs et des princes Russes, le Roi de Bavière, Le Roi du Portugal, le Prince de Galles, des hommes politiques Français… Piètre actrice peut-être mais quelle organisation et quel chemin parcouru en quelques années.

Le carnet de 1894, alors qu'elle n'a que 21 ans est une longue suite de chiffres et un vrai catalogue de Joaillier où figure le prix la description, la taille des pierres et parfois le poids des bijoux offerts par ses protecteurs. Hortense est ambitieuse, je découvre qu'elle prend des cours de Russe, et que son premier investissement, avec l'argent gagné « allongée », est d'apprendre à lire et à écrire. 1901, elle part en Russie quelques mois et en revient définitivement riche, à l'abri de tous besoins. D'autres livres de comptes cachés dans le cabinet de toilette m'apprennent où cet argent est placé : dans les chemins de fer Français et en appartements, elle refuse de souscrire aux emprunts Russes ! Trop loin, elle veut garder un œil sur ses investissements.

Apprenant à la connaître je prends l'habitude de soulever chaque latte de parquet, chaque tapis, de vérifier les ourlets, d'inspecter les vases, les creux, les bosses, les pages des livres ! Je me lance dans une véritable course au trésor. Chaque objet découvert, même si il est sans valeur me cause une joie enfantine. J'arrête d'aller travailler, obsédée par Hortense.

Par contre aucune trace de sa fille, ni sur les photos, ni dans ses carnets. Je me demande si Violette a tout détruit ou si c'est cette indifférence, qui l'a poussé à dresser ce mur entre le souvenir et elle ? Un soir, alors que j'explore une table de nuit, je découvre dissimulé, sous la tablette de marbre, un paquet de lettres. Cent soixante-douze lettres d'amour et 3 photos d'un bel officier d'une trentaine d'années à la moustache conquérante. Il est aviateur. Ils s'écriront du 5 février 1913 au 28 décembre 1916. Sur l'une des photos il pose devant son avion, plus jeune qu'Hortense, je comprends qu'il est le père de Violette. Nouée par un ruban, une lettre courte, datée du 3 janvier 1917, d'un camarade aviateur, apprend à Hortense que Louis Goldstein est mort au combat. C'est d'ailleurs à cette date que s'arrêtent tous les carnets d'Hortense, comme si compter, entasser, ordonner et trier n'avait plus d'importance désormais.

Petit Rat

ADRIA J. CIMINO

"*Pirouette piquée* and *encore* and *encore* and *piquée arabesque.*" *Madame* Martin's voice was in my head, guiding me as usual as I crossed the floor, but my body wasn't obeying. "*Détends les bras*, Odile! Relax your arms. *Allez, recommence!* Start over. *Un, deux, trois, quatre, cinq, six, sept et huit… et un…*" *Madame* Martin counted, clapped her hands and frowned as my second attempt was about as bad as the first.

"I'm sorry," I whispered, half to my teacher, half to myself as I hurried to the door. Class was over, and for once in my 13-year-old life, I was relieved.

"Odile, wait." I felt *Madame* Martin's hand on my arm and turned around.

The studio had already emptied.

I panicked. She was going to tell me I couldn't be part of the demonstrations next month on the stage of the Opera Garnier. She would be right, too, but the idea was so awful that tears already gathered in the corners of my eyes.

Madame Martin didn't say anything like that.

"I know what happened with your sister is weighing

on you," she said. "It's normal."

Her warm brown eyes comforted me, and I blinked back my tears. I didn't know what to say or do other than nod my head in agreement. She squeezed my hand.

"You are a talented dancer, Odile. If you weren't, you would not be a *petit rat*. You would not be here at all."

But Odette was talented too. More than me. I'd overheard Mom and Dad talking after one of our medical exams. Our identical twin backs were equally flexible and our twin hips gave us the same turnout. But Odette had a gracefulness that even an identical body like mine couldn't copy. That was OK. I didn't mind being one step below my sister on the ballet ladder. I didn't mind that she passed to the higher division last year while I stayed back.

After all, just being accepted at the Paris Opera's *Ecole de Danse* was enough to make me happy with this body of mine for the rest of my life.

Odette and I had been here more than two years, but our ballet story started a lot earlier.

It was simple: Right from the start, we were meant to be dancers.

Mom went into labor during *Swan Lake*, rushing out as the Prince betrayed his beloved Odette. Six hours later, Mom was holding two screaming babies in her arms and named them Odette and Odile.

So now, as I stood facing *Madame* Martin and my own sweaty body in the mirror, what was I going to say? That what was meant to happen wasn't going to happen and that totally wasn't fair? That if Odette couldn't be a dancer, maybe I shouldn't either? All that had been going through my mind during each pirouette, each *jeté*.

And those thoughts stayed there. In my head.

"You don't need extra rehearsal or time in the studio before demonstrations, Odile. You aren't falling out of pirouettes because of a problem with alignment. You are making errors because of what's going on up here." She tapped her hand against her smooth forehead. "You need to accept the situation as it is and make the best of it."

I nodded and kept my eyes on the frayed edges of my ballet slippers.

"Odette, it's me, pick up," I whispered.

"Shouldn't you be in class now?"

"I left a few minutes earlier. I feel sick…"

"Liar!" Her sharp words cut me off. "Don't screw up your career, Odile." I could almost see her on the other end of the line, the mirror reflection of myself: Curly blonde hair stretched flat into a bun, blue eyes with that funny brown spot on the right one.

But the mirror stopped there. She wouldn't be wearing a damp light-blue leotard like me. She wouldn't even be wearing a dance T-shirt. I was sure she'd boycotted every one we owned. Probably hiding in jeans and some baggy old shirt.

"I didn't call to talk about me," I said. "I just… wanted to know how your knee is doing."

"What difference does it make? I'm not coming back. We both know it!"

I didn't want to think of the injury. But I couldn't help it. Every time I heard my sister's voice, a series of scary pictures flashed through my mind. It was my imagination, because I wasn't there when it happened. Sometimes imagination is worse than reality. I saw Odette's knee buckle, saw the pain in the face that looked like mine, heard her scream turn to a quiet cry. Sometimes I could even feel the pain in my own knee.

The doctor tried to make us feel better, saying that at our age, the body's power to heal is amazing. But he was honest: Sure, Odette would be able to dance again, but not at the level needed to make it through our school and into the world's top ballet companies. Some girls hid blisters so they could continue pointe work. I'd done it plenty of times. If we were afraid a few days to heal a blister would set us back, how could Odette ever come back after months out? And with a knee that wouldn't ever be the same.

In a matter of two days, she went from being the star of her division to packing her bags and enrolling in the local middle school down the street from our apartment.

"You'll still be able to dance." I tried to make my words encouraging, but I sounded pretty pathetic. That's probably why Odette's most recent reactions to me were rolling her eyes or walking away.

"Do we have to talk about this again, Odile? The accident happened two months ago, so get over it." Her voice didn't sound as gruff as she wanted it to sound. It just sounded sad.

"Let's go to *Flore* for hot chocolate when I come home this weekend, OK?" I pleaded with her. Our old routine from last winter.

I could see her shrugging her shoulders, shaking her head.

"Maybe."

Silence for a minute and then her voice again.

"Your second ballet class starts in a few minutes, Odile. You'd better hurry."

My best friend Sarah and I executed perfect *révérences* as the school's director passed with a few adults in street clothes. They admired us and our polite, ballerina curtsies. We played along, smiling as we stretched on the huge swirl of spiral steps in the five minutes before class.

Sarah reached over and smoothed a rebellious lock of hair that had popped through my hair net.

"Hold on, I got it," she said, wiggling the loose pin.

"Thanks." My eyes went back to their faraway place.

"How's Odette?" she asked, as if reading my mind.

"Awful. I just got off the phone with her. She'll hardly talk to me…"

"Yeah, it's really unfair. I mean, especially since she was so good."

"I know, I know."

"I'm sorry." Sarah put an arm around me and leaned close so her silky dark bun touched my fuzzy blonde one.

And then we were in class, part of the wave of leotards moving into the massive studio. At the *barre*, I tried to forget about Odette, about injury, about everything.

When I got home Friday night, Odette wasn't there.

"Where is she?" I asked, dropping my bag on the floor of our room.

Mom followed me inside and sat on Odette's bed. She looked like an older version of us, with the curly hair set free instead of trapped in a bun.

"She's spending the weekend with Grandma and Grandpa in Normandy."

"What?"

I was furious. What right did she have to take off like that? I wouldn't see her for another week.

"She could have at least told me!"

"Odile, you and your sister aren't connected at the hip! You have the right to live your own lives and make your own plans. When you were both at the school, doing everything together was almost natural, but now that Odette is at home…"

"Fine, whatever." I didn't want to hear any more. I didn't want to see things had changed. I didn't want to see I was on my own. Before, it used to be a threesome: ballet, Odette and me. Now it was ballet and me. Could I do it alone? And was it fair to my sister if I did? She deserved it more.

"She doesn't want to see me," I finally said, sinking onto the bed that was mine, but felt foreign.

"I think she needs some space," Mom said. "It's hard for her to accept what happened of course."

"Yeah, and to see her less-talented sister continue while she can't."

"Don't say that, Odile! Your sister wants you to continue, and you know it! She wants you to stop fretting about her and to focus on what you have to do. Which brings me to the subject…"

"What subject?" My heart was pounding a mile a minute.

"The school is being very accommodating, Odile. I spoke with the director this week. They aren't interested in sending you away even though it's clear you're having difficulty. The concern is you will send yourself away. If you continue to let yourself slip, what will happen during your evaluation? The decision is in your hands. You're a smart girl. You have more control over your own destiny than you think."

I swallowed hard. I knew everything my mom said, everything the director said, was true.

That weekend, I went to *Flore* alone and sipped hot chocolate. I sat upstairs in the quiet room we would always go to, and I thought back to our conversations. We talked about ballet. Period. I guess it really was my life. But it was Odette's life too. What did that mean for her now? A tear fell into my drink, making a round glossy spot in all of that frothy cocoa.

"Glissade, pas de chat, allez, pas de chat, plus haut… Energie, Odile! Mathilde, *les bras…"*

I threw myself into the movement this time as

Mathilde and I moved across the floor. I forgot about everything except the music that carried us like two dancing leaves. Better, but still not my best.

Then pirouettes, one of my old strong points. I tapped my pointe shoe nervously against the floor as I gripped the *barre* with one hand. Why was it scarier to try something I was usually good at than something super difficult? I didn't have time to answer. It was my turn. One, two, three... I should've been on a roll by now. I should've had my confidence back. And then, a fleeting image of myself—of my sister—in the mirror. I fell out of the pirouette.

"Shit," I whispered.

Because of what's going on up here. In my mind, I could see *Madame* Martin tapping her forehead and saying those words.

Class was over. Our last movement was the usual *révérence.* Then, I pulled off my pointe shoes, stuffed my sore toes into sneakers and ran for the door.

My reflection was waiting for me. Me, without the ballet look. Her hair was in a ponytail, and she wore jeans and a brown suede jacket.

"Odette, what are you doing here?" I threw my arms open, and she let me hug her for the quickest second on earth. Then she took a step back.

"I'm here to save your ass."

"What do you mean?"

She grabbed my arm and practically dragged me down the stairs to a quiet corner. On the way, she nodded and smiled at old friends, but didn't let up the pace for anyone.

We sat by a bay window overlooking the lawn.

"I still don't know why you're here."

"Yes you do."

"OK, to tell me you should be here instead of me, I suck and should be home. You saw my pirouettes! Don't lie, Odette!"

She rolled her eyes. Words didn't easily hurt my sister.

"You don't suck. You're not focusing any more. It's as simple as that. And you know what? That's just as bad. That's what I came here to tell you."

I bit my lip and tried to look away. But I couldn't. Odette was my mirror, showing me the truth. Whether I wanted to see it or not.

But was I strong enough to accept it?

We sat there cross-legged on the ground, facing each other for I don't know how long. She wouldn't tell me what she'd been doing. She just kept repeating what *I* should be doing: going to class, forgetting about the past and thinking only about my future.

I thought of my sister's visit while I tossed and turned that night. I thought about her again as I groggily danced the next day. And my dancing was better. Strangely, I leaped into the air with loads of energy, glided across the room with grace.

"*Très bien*, Odile," *Madame* Martin said, her eyes glowing.

I kept that feeling in my heart and tried to preserve it as if it were in a glass jar.

That day passed and then the next and the next. I was getting stronger again. So strong, that on Friday night, on my way home from school, I stopped to see our old dance teacher on rue de Courcelles.

And that's when I saw Odette. She was working, slowly but steadily, with Liliane. Liliane was gentle and calm. The perfect person to bring a dancer back to life. I hung back in the shadows, watching my sister wince as she turned painful pirouettes on demi pointe. I knew she wouldn't be back to pointe work any time soon. She wouldn't be back to the *Ecole de Danse* either.

But she was back to dance. And that made me smile. I smiled because, even though her body ached, I knew her heart didn't. I could see it in her face as she danced. To me, she looked as beautiful and graceful as ever.

I didn't dare interrupt. When we sat opposite each other at dinner that night, I didn't tell her that I'd stopped by, that I'd seen her dance. If I did, she would be angry. My parents didn't seem to know what she'd been up to either. I don't think they would have been too happy about it. The doctor had been really cautious, saying she shouldn't even get near a dance studio for six months. But with Liliane, my sister was in good hands. I would keep her secret.

Backstage at the Opera Garnier. Hustle and bustle. Demonstrations of what we'd learned these past months and years. Mathilde, Sarah and I went through *pliés* and *relevés* at the *barre*. The three of us would be traveling across the stage together in a series of *petits sauts* and turns.

A familiar voice startled me as I laughed at Mathilde's silly joke. Odette. Not just anyone could get backstage before the show. But who could refuse Odette? I think our teachers cried even more than my sister on the day she left the school.

I hadn't seen her in weeks. Every time I came home for a weekend, she had run off here or there with some excuse. I told myself she was secretly dancing and that made me feel better.

I'd called to invite her to demonstrations, but she'd never answered my call. I left a jumbled sort of message asking her to come but saying I wouldn't be mad if she didn't. So maybe she thought I didn't want her there. I expressed my feelings better through dance than through words.

And then there she was, smiling in the shadows a few feet away. I hurried over to her. This time, when I hugged her, she hugged me back.

"Why didn't you tell me? I didn't think you'd come!"

"Don't cry! Your makeup's going to run." Odette shot me a half smile. Her eyes were sparkling almost as much as before.

"Listen," she continued. "I wanted time… to work things out. There are some things we have to do alone, Odile, not as twins."

"Are you dancing?" I hoped she would tell me.

She nodded.

"Not like before… But saying it's all or nothing was stupid. One day, I went to Liliane's and tried. I missed it so much. It doesn't matter as much that I'm not going to be on this stage, Odile. If I can still dance even a little, I'll be OK."

There was so much I wanted to say, but the show was about to start. I squeezed my sister's hand and left her waiting in the wings.

Le Chemin du Dragon

Didier Quémener

"There are mysteries which men can only guess at, which age by age they may solve only in part."
Abraham Stoker

April 8, 1818: 39th section of Père-Lachaise cemetery.
(Russian accent)
I can't believe they put me here. They will pay dearly for this…

A few months later: 19th section of Père-Lachaise cemetery, Chemin du Dragon.
(Russian accent)
What was I telling you? Let the game begin…

During the month of May, 2018: 10th section of Père-Lachaise cemetery, Chemin Denon.
Anatole could almost hear the final notes of the Nocturne in B-flat minor, Opus 9, Number 1 as he approached the tomb. He knew every nuance, every

detail of the music by heart. The long hours of research involving complex compositions and the weeks of rehearsal alone at his piano reached a crescendo: The day of the competition to win a spot at the conservatory. Now, wasn't he obliged to come here and pay tribute?

With a sense of sadness, Anatole lowered his head and looked at the statue of Euterpe on Chopin's tomb. In his mind, he started a conversation about the greatness of the pianist.

"Like you, I would have loved to have known him," Anatole said as he addressed the statue of the muse of music. "He could have taught me so much, and I would have told him all that I feel every time my fingers touch the keys and bring his music back to life… Like you, my heart is elsewhere, and like you, my dreams are set to music."

"It's certainly not the time to start whining in front of a block of stone!" a voice whispered.

Anatole froze. He suddenly felt colder than the flowers at the statue's foot as the gusts of early spring wind tossed them about.

"I'm tired, that's all," he said to himself. "These past few months of burning the candle at both ends…"

"What are you waiting for?"

Annoyance quickly replaced astonishment.

"I'm not here to offer etiquette lessons, but you should know that this isn't a place to disturb people," Anatole said, abruptly turning around.

But he faced no one. Only the wind from time to time, a gray cat crossing the path, trees, cobblestones… There wasn't a single person in the area.

"Who are you?" Anatole called out, turning around and peering left and right. "Why are you hiding? What do you want? And what's with the Russian accent?"

Silence. Feeling ridiculous, Anatole rubbed his hand against his forehead and took in a deep breath.

The voice resonated through the air once again.

"Well, don't just stand there! Hurry up! I'm waiting for you…"

As if hypnotized, Anatole decided to play along. Curiosity had overtaken his feelings of disbelief.

"OK, fine. You be the guide, and I'll follow your instructions. It seems like that's your style." He couldn't hide the sarcasm in his voice.

"Exactly! Meet me in the nineteenth section of the cemetery. It's along the Chemin du Dragon."

Anatole tossed one last look at the statue and strode toward the meeting spot.

The air became gloomier with each step as he followed the twisted, descending paths. Drawings of bats and other creatures covered tombs and rusted metal doors.

"It feels like Dracula is right here in Paris on the Chemin du Dragon," Anatole murmured as he maintained his rapid pace.

"You're almost there!" The woman's voice had returned.

"Which tomb?" He nearly spat out the words.

"Tomb? What an insult! A mausoleum, my dear. A marble temple supported by ten columns. And all perfectly adapted to my eccentric demands!"

A few feet away, Anatole spotted the imposing structure that overlooked practically the entire cemetery. At its base was the entrance to a crypt.

"So, are you going to tell me your name? You obviously already know mine…"

"Finally!" she said. "We're finally getting to the heart of the matter. I'm Countess Marie-Elisabeth Demidov. My closest friends know me as Princess Alexandrovna Stroganov, wife of Count Nicolas Demidov. I am an aristocrat and very proud of my social status!"

Anatole looked at the staircase leading to the stone

structure, and his eyes moved upward to an inscription surrounded by torches and sculptures of ermines and wolves:

Here lies Elisabeth Demidov, born Baronne de Stroganov. Deceased the 8th of April, 1818.

"Aristocrat?" Anatole laughed. "My dear lady, the aristocracy was buried long ago—probably around the same time as you!"

Air vents constructed into the stone structure caught Anatole's eye, and he couldn't help commenting with irony, "It looks like you're expecting visitors? It seems those holes are to let fresh air into the tomb… You usually don't see that kind of thing around here."

"Are you the only one who doesn't know about the legend?"

"Legends are to adults what bedtime stories are to children."

"You certainly won't be so smug in a few minutes. That, I can guarantee."

The countess paused and then continued, "Please know, my dear, that many are those who see in the steps a direct access to hell and this place is none other than the entry gates. But let's leave that to amuse the curious. There is a much more interesting story to be told."

Anatole made his way to the top of the steps and listened attentively, as if under a spell.

"According to the legend, the princess—that's my ego and me," she said, laughing. "I'll begin again: The legend says that in my will, I offer my fortune to the person who spends three hundred and sixty five days and three hundred and sixty six nights by my side in the crypt. Of course, the person cannot leave for any reason… I love loyalty from my admirers, especially when it comes to them watching over my eternal beauty!

Anyone can try his luck. The only rule: Don't leave me for even an instant."

"Were you successful? That crazy request must have attracted candidates who were just as eccentric as you."

"Absolutely," the countess said. "I've lost count of those who heard of the famous clause in my will, moved in and tried to win my treasures. Sadly, however, all who tried never lasted more than one night! Some have died, God rest their souls. Others simply went insane… The most recent left with quite worrisome testimony (my personal touch!) Did they really see phantoms, vampires or demons as many believe? Or were they simply hallucinations caused by the mushroom spores in the crypt? The mystery remains unsolved." A long, icy laugh.

Anatole remained silent for several minutes. The story repeated itself in his head as night began to fall.

"The cemetery is already closed, and the guards are going to start their rounds," the countess said. "You must hurry or they will find you and put you out."

"Hurry to do what?" Anatole asked, returning to the present. "Your story might have fascinated the naïve and incited curiosity for two hundred years, but I'm one of the skeptics, *Madame*. I have much more important things to do than hang around here and talk to myself."

His firm tone could no longer hide his exasperation and desire to leave the place as soon as possible.

"Wait, Anatoly, wait… Come here, through the right side. There is an opening. I will guide you."

Anatoly. Why did she call me that? he asked himself. *Probably more of her bizarre behavior.*

"Your fortune doesn't interest me," he said aloud. "And even if it did, what is really left of your riches after all these years? Maybe enough to pay for a coffee at the café across the street?"

"You shouldn't underestimate my words, Anatoly," sighed the countess. "On the right, near the third column, if you lift the debris from the stone and cement, you will find a key that will offer you access to the crypt. Now hurry! There isn't a moment to lose."

"Anatole, my name is Anatole—not Anatoly! If what you said is true, I understand why no one was able to put up with you for more than a few hours, or even worse, a few days! But I have principles. And as a consequence, I will force myself to remain courteous. I'll take the key—that is, if it exists. I'll open the doors, and then I'll let out a couple of screams and close the doors. Is that what you're looking for? Yes, in my opinion. Then I'll dispose of the key far from this place so you'll never bother anyone again."

As if his legs were mechanically guided, Anatole made his way toward the stones and dust. He lifted the cement block that wasn't any bigger than his hand and discovered a long, slim key, worn by age.

"Miraculous that it's still here," he murmured.

"I've been guarding it," said the countess. "Go ahead, enter…"

Anatole inserted the key in the door situated around the back of the gigantic structure and pushed the handle warped by time and lack of use.

"Careful on those steps! They are slippery and crooked."

"I noticed, but thanks anyway," Anatole said, shaking his head.

"Use your cell phone as a torch, Anatoly."

"I don't have one," he snapped.

"You don't have a cell phone? Well, isn't that something? Nowadays, everyone has one. That's all right. You will simply follow my instructions to the letter…"

After descending a dozen steps, which seemed to take an eternity, Anatole arrived at his destination. The humid scent of mold filled the crypt and made him sneeze several times.

The countess guided his steps.

"Listen carefully, my child. Take one step to your left."

Anatole obeyed.

"Extend your arms. Do you feel the rock?"

"Yes." His voice had become childlike.

"Push with all of your might to move it to the other side."

Anatole placed his hands on the rock.

"Go ahead, use a little strength!" the countess said, laughing.

A deafening sound resonated in the profound corner of the crypt. As if he knew what to do without further instruction, Anatole rubbed the spot where the rock had been. He felt a rough, metallic surface.

"We've made it, Anatoly. Now it's your turn to play!"

Blindly, Anatole felt the edges of the steel safe. Powdery rust covered his hands before he reached a vent that allowed him to lift the lid. A squeaking sound and then bits of stone falling and rolling across the floor. Anatole had the strange feeling he was about to face his destiny.

"Be careful. They are fragile."

"What? What is fragile?"

"Go ahead. Take them—but gently."

Anatole's eyes had started to adjust to the dimness. He plunged one hand into the open safe. His heart was beating a mile a minute.

"But what is…"

He stopped midsentence. Then he continued, nearly shouting.

"Incredible! How did you… I mean, where did you get these?"

"Astonishing, isn't it?" the countess replied. "I knew you would love them. I'm quite proud of myself."

"It's not possible! This has to be some kind of joke.

We thought they were destroyed. No one suspected they still existed."

Anatole thoroughly searched the safe with nervous hands.

"Caution, Anatoly! Don't forget they have been waiting untouched for you for more than one hundred and fifty years."

Reality caught up with Anatole, and a mountain of questions grew in his mind.

"I'm listening," he said. "Why should I bother asking questions? You owe me more than a few simple explanations, don't you?"

"Anatoly, my Anatoly… I so would love to hold you in my arms and share all of my happiness with you. I call you Anatoly for a simple reason: You remind me of my youngest son, who also was named Anatole."

"I understand, but I'm not the only one in the world with that name. Anatole, Anatoly… What's the connection with your son?"

"Patience, and you'll find out," said the countess. "You don't already understand? You don't see? I'll explain: My son Anatoly knew Frédéric. They were about the same age and became dear friends."

"You mean Frédéric Chopin?"

"The one and only Fryderyk Franciszek Szopen, indeed. Did you notice my imitation of the Polish accent? Pretty good, isn't it? Ah, what a composer… Well, I don't have to convince you of that. Did you ever ask yourself why you have such passion for his work?"

"No… No, but…"

The countess interrupted.

"What you hold in your hands is worth more than gold in my eyes, and I'm sure it is the same from your point of view. Do you realize what this means? His art, his greatness, will finally be reborn through your hands! A short time before his death in our great city of Paris, he had given Anatoly all of his latest work and uncompleted symphonies. As you said, everyone thought they had been destroyed, even to this day."

Anatole remained frozen, holding the precious sheets of music to his chest.

"When I found myself here, Anatoly started the famous legend about my crypt with the hope of one day attracting the person meant to discover these masterpieces. As I mentioned, Frédéric gave them to Anatoly shortly before his death, and Anatoly had the excellent idea of leaving them here with me for safekeeping at the Père-Lachaise cemetery. When I saw you in front of Chopin's tomb earlier, I knew that we were almost there and the magic of Frédéric would live once again."

A long moment of silence and then the countess spoke.

"Say something, my boy!"

"I… I don't know… I no longer know what to say! Everything is so confusing, and at the same time, clear. It's as if my life collapsed around me in a fraction of a second and magically rebuilt itself. I'm filled with pride, responsibility, spirituality. It seems normal, yet incredible!"

"That is to be expected, my child." The countess' voice was gentle. "Come along. Take the music and close the safe. It's time for you to leave and set to work with these beautiful musical notes that await you! I'm sure you are impatient to discover them on your piano. You shall see: The final mazurkas are exceptional!"

Almost instinctively, Anatole followed the countess' instructions and closed the door of the crypt.

"Keep the key, my Anatoly. Keep it as a souvenir of our meeting and the bond that unites us now and for eternity."

Anatole slipped the key into his pocket, placed the

sheet music in his bag and walked toward the exit of the cemetery with peace in his heart.

"Visit him once again, my child, after you study the music. You owe him that. After all, you and Frédéric were such dear friends…"

The May breeze ruffled his hair. Anatole looked up at the Parisian sky at dusk. He climbed up the low wall and jumped over the gate to rue du Repos. With a light step, he walked along boulevard de Ménilmontant. The City of Light had never before looked so beautiful.

Le Chemin du Dragon

DIDIER QUÉMENER

"There are mysteries which men can only guess at,
which age by age they may solve only in part."
Abraham Stoker

8 avril MDCCCXVIII : 39ème division.

(accent russe)

*« Je n'arrive pas à croire qu'ils m'aient mis ici ! Ils me le
paieront cher… »*

Des mois plus tard : 19ème division, Chemin du Dragon.

(accent russe)

« Qu'est-ce que je vous disais ? Que le spectacle commence… »

Pendant le mois de mai MMXVIII : 10ème division,
Chemin Denon.

Anatole pouvait presque entendre les dernières notes
de la Nocturne en Si bémol mineur, Op. 9, No.1 en

s'approchant du tombeau. Il connaissait l'œuvre sur le bout des doigts. Des longues heures de recherche musicale sur des partitions complexes, aux semaines de répétitions, seul devant son piano, pour finalement aboutir à la délivrance le jour du concours d'entrée au conservatoire. Après tout, c'était comme une sorte d'obligation morale que de lui rendre hommage.

Austère, triste et tête baissée, Anatole fixait la statue d'Euterpe. Il s'imagina une conversation sur la grandeur du pianiste.

— Comme toi j'aurais tant aimé le connaître ! Qu'il m'apprenne sa virtuosité, que je lui dise toute l'émotion ressentie lorsque mes mains se posent sur l'ébène et l'ivoire pour faire revire l'une de ses compositions… soupira-t-il. Comme toi mon cœur est ailleurs, comme toi je rêve en musique romantique !

— Ce n'est certainement pas le moment de se larmoyer devant un morceau de pierre ! une voix chuchota.

Plus que la bourrasque de vent qui caressait les premières fleurs printanières repiquées devant le médaillon du profil gauche de la statue, Anatole se sentit soudainement glacé et paralysé.

— La fatigue. Ce n'est que le surmenage des derniers mois… se dit-il.

— Alors, qu'est-ce que tu attends ?

L'agacement l'emporta vite sur l'étonnement. Anatole se retourna brusquement.

— Je vais vous apprendre la politesse moi ! On ne dérange pas… s'interrompit-il, bouche bée.

Personne. Toujours le vent par intermittence, un chat gris qui traversait, des arbres, des pavés. Mais personne aux alentours.

— Qui êtes-vous ? Pourquoi vous cacher ? Que voulez-vous ? Quel est cet accent russe si fort et si désagréable ? lança Anatole à voix haute, tournant sur lui-même plusieurs fois.

Le silence.

Se sentant ridicule pour un instant, Anatole passa la main sur son front et prit une longue inspiration.

La voix résonna une nouvelle fois.

— Allons, ne reste pas là sans rien faire ! Dépêche-toi, je t'attends…

Hypnotisé, Anatole décida de se laisser prendre au jeu. La curiosité l'emportait sur la stupéfaction.

— Très bien, dites-moi : vous allez me guider et je suis vos indications, c'est ainsi que l'on communique tous les deux ? interrogea Anatole d'un ton légèrement sarcastique.

— Exactement ! Rendez-vous à la 19ème division, Chemin du Dragon.

Anatole jeta un dernier coup d'œil à la statue et se dirigea d'un pas ferme au lieu donné. Redescendant allées et chemins tortueux, le décor devenait de plus en plus glauque : des tombeaux, sépultures et portes métalliques rouillées étaient recouverts de chauve-souris et autres créatures frissonnantes.

— Le Comte Dracula en plein Paris dans le Chemin du Dragon ? dit-il dans un murmure. Rien de plus normal !

Il ralentit le pas.

— Tu y es presque, reprit la voix féminine.

— Quelle tombe ? demanda sèchement Anatole.

— Tombe ? Quel affront ! Un mausolée mon cher, un temple de marbre soutenu par dix colonnes, le tout parfaitement adapté à mon excentricité !

A quelques pas de là, Anatole aperçut l'imposant monument qui surplombait tout le cimetière, ainsi que l'entrée d'un caveau.

— Votre nom peut-être ? Puisque de toute évidence vous connaissez déjà le mien à en entendre ce ton familier à mon égard !

— Parfait, on entre dans le vif du sujet : il était temps ! ajouta la voix empressée. Comtesse Marie-Elisabeth Demidov, Princesse Alexandrovna Stroganov pour les intimes, épouse du Comte Nicolas Demidov. Aristocrate et fière de l'être !

Encadré de torchères, décoré de sculptures plus étranges les unes que les autres où se mêlaient hermines, marteaux, têtes de loups rehaussées de nœuds, Anatole pouvait lire en haut des larges escaliers qui menaient à l'édifice l'inscription suivante :

Ici reposent les cendres d'Elisabeth Demidov, née Baronne de Stroganov. Décédée le 8 avril 1818.

— Aristocrate ? s'amusa Anatole. Ma chère amie, il y a bien longtemps que l'aristocratie a été enterrée avec vous !

Son regard s'arrêta sur des trous d'aération taillés directement dans la pierre brute. Intrigué, Anatole ne put s'empêcher d'ironiser.

— Vous attendiez de la visite on dirait ? Les ouvertures là, c'est pour laisser passer l'air frais depuis l'intérieur du tombeau ? Ce n'est pas courant !

Aussitôt, la Comtesse lui répondit.

— En plein dans le mille ! Serais-tu le seul à ignorer mes légendes ?

— Les légendes sont aux adultes ce que les histoires du soir sont aux enfants avant de se coucher… rétorqua Anatole du tac-au-tac.

— Tu feras moins le malin dans quelques minutes, je te le garantis !

La Comtesse fit une pause et commença son récit :

— Sache, mon cher et tendre, que nombreux sont ceux qui voient en ces escaliers un accès direct aux enfers et que ce lieu ne serait rien d'autre que leurs portes d'entrée. Mais laissons cela pour amuser les curieux, voici ce qui est bien plus intéressant pour toi !

Anatole se trouvait en haut des marches et écouta attentivement, comme envoûté.

— La légende raconte que la Princesse, c'est-à-dire moi et mon ego ! dit-elle en riant. Donc je reprends : la légende dit que j'avais déposé mon testament chez un notaire de Paris pour léguer la totalité de ma fortune à la personne de bonne volonté qui consentirait, pendant 365 jours et 366 nuits, à s'enfermer auprès de moi dans la solitude et froideur de mon caveau. Mais surtout à ne s'en éloigner sous aucun prétexte : j'aime que l'on veille sur ma beauté éternelle sans interruption ! Quiconque pouvait tenter sa chance : peu importe vos occupations mais il ne fallait point me quitter un seul instant !

— Avez-vous rencontré du succès ? s'enquit Anatole, distrait par cette histoire. Cette demande farfelue a certainement éveillé l'intérêt de personnages tout autant singuliers que vous puissiez l'être !

— Absolument ! dit la Comtesse d'une voix joyeuse. Je ne compte plus à ce jour les personnes ayant entendu parler de cette fameuse clause et qui voulurent s'approprier les lieux en quête de mon héritage. Hélas, hélas, hélas… Tous ceux qui ont essayé n'ont pas pu tenir plus d'une nuit ! Certains sont morts, paix à leurs âmes, d'autres sont devenus fous. Les derniers en sont revenus avec des témoignages inquiétants : ma touche personnelle ! Ont-ils réellement vu des fantômes, des vampires ou bien encore des démons comme semble le croire pas mal de monde ? Ou alors ont-ils simplement eu des hallucinations provoquées par les spores des champignons qui grandissent dans la crypte ? Le mystère reste entier ! conclut-elle dans un rire long et glacial.

Anatole resta muet pendant quelques minutes. Le récit retentissait encore dans sa tête alors que la nuit commençait à tomber lentement.

— Le cimetière est déjà fermé et ils vont commencer

leurs rondes, reprit la Comtesse. Tu dois te dépêcher sinon les gardiens vont te trouver et te reconduire à l'extérieur.

— Me dépêcher de faire quoi ? dit-il reprenant ses esprits. Vos histoires à dormir debout ont pu fasciner des naïfs et faire vivre une croyance pendant près de deux cents ans mais je fais partie des sceptiques moi Madame et j'ai des choses bien plus importantes à faire que de rester là, en train de parler dans le vide à voix haute !

Le ton ferme d'Anatole ne dissimulait plus son agacement ni son désir de quitter les lieux.

— Attends Anatoly, attends… Passe sur le côté droit, il y a une ouverture : je vais te guider ! semblait crier la voix de la Comtesse.

— Anatoly ? Pourquoi m'appelle-t-elle ainsi ? s'interrogea-t-il. Encore une de ses lubies ! en déduisit Anatole.

— Je ne suis pas cupide. Votre fortune ne m'intéresse pas. Et quand bien même fut-ce le cas, après autant d'années, que reste-t-il vraiment de cette richesse ? Tout juste de quoi se payer un crème au café d'en face ? ironisa-t-il.

— Tu ne devrais pas sous-estimer mes mots Anatoly… soupira la Comtesse. Sur la droite près de la troisième colonne, en soulevant les débris de ciment et de pierre, tu trouveras une clef qui donne accès au caveau : presse-toi !

— Anatole, mon prénom c'est Anatole : non pas Anatoly ! Si vos dires sont authentiques, je comprends mieux à présent pourquoi jamais personne n'a eu la force de vous supporter plus de quelques heures ou bien pire encore, quelques jours ! répondit-il d'un ton sec, sans ménagement. Je suis une personne de conviction et, à tort ou à raison, j'ai des principes. Par conséquent, je vais m'efforcer de rester courtois : je prends cette clef, à supposer qu'elle existe réellement, j'ouvre les portes, j'expire deux ou trois cris d'étonnement ou de crainte et je referme les portes. Est-ce suffisant ? A mon avis, je crois que oui. Ensuite je jette la clef loin de ces lieux pour que vous ne dérangiez plus personne ! termina-t-il en s'approchant de la colonne.

Machinalement, Anatole avança vers le petit monticule de pierres, de lichens et de poussière. Il souleva les morceaux de ciment qui n'étaient pas plus gros que la taille d'une main, et mis à jour une longue clef fine rongée par le temps.

— C'est un miracle qu'elle soit toujours là ! dit-il à voix basse.

— J'y veille ! dit la Comtesse. Allons, entre…

Devant l'entrée du caveau située à l'arrière du gigantesque édifice, Anatole n'hésita pas un seul instant pour introduire la clef et forcer la porte de droite grippée par le temps et l'immobilité de ces dernières années.

— Attention aux marches : elles sont glissantes et irrégulières.

— J'avais remarqué, merci tout de même ! répondit Anatole en secouant la tête.

— Utilise ton portable comme lampe de poche Anatoly, lui lança la Comtesse, ce sera plus sage.

— Je n'en ai pas ! répliqua-t-il aussitôt froidement.

— Pas de portable ? Non mais c'est un comble ! Serais-tu le seul à ne pas en posséder de nos jours ? Ce n'est pas grave, tu vas suivre mes indications à la lettre.

Après une dizaine de marches qui parurent une éternité, Anatole arriva à destination. L'odeur humide des moisissures qui emplissait le fond du caveau le fit éternuer plusieurs fois.

La Comtesse conduisait ses pas :

— Ecoute-moi bien mon garçon, avance d'un pas sur ta gauche…

Anatole obéissait sans faire de commentaire.

— Tends le bras : tu sens ce bloc de pierre ?

— Oui ? dit-il d'une voix d'enfant.

— Pousse le très fort devant toi pour le faire basculer de l'autre côté !

Anatole posa ses deux mains sur la pierre à hauteur de son buste.

— Allez, un peu de vigueur ! ricanait la Comtesse.

Un bruit sourd résonna dans les profondeurs du caveau. Comme s'il savait ce qu'il devait faire sans plus aucune indication, Anatole frotta le socle où reposait le bloc de plusieurs kilos. Il sentit une surface métallique et rugueuse.

— Nous y sommes Anatoly : c'est à toi de jouer !

A l'aveugle, Anatole caressa du bout des doigts les bords du coffre d'acier. Il sentit une rouille poudreuse recouvrant ses mains puis une fente lui permettant de soulever le couvercle. Un léger grincement sec, de petits morceaux de pierre tombant et roulant sur le sol alors que le dessus basculait vers le haut et Anatole avait l'étrange impression de se trouver face à son destin.

— Sois prudent, ils sont fragiles…

— Quoi ? dit-il finalement après de longues minutes de silence. Qu'est-ce qui est fragile ?

— Vas-y : prends-en un délicatement.

Les yeux d'Anatole commencèrent à s'accommoder lentement de cette obscurité. Il plongea la main dans le coffre ouvert. Son cœur palpitait d'excitation.

— Mais qu'est-ce que…

Il s'arrêta au milieu de sa phrase. Puis il reprit, presque en hurlant :

— Incroyable ! Comment avez-vous… Enfin je veux dire, où les avez-vous eues ?

— Etonnant, n'est-ce pas ? lui répondit la Comtesse. Je savais que ça te plairait : je suis fière de moi !

— Ce n'est pas possible, c'est une plaisanterie ! Nous les croyions détruites… Personne n'en soupçonnait l'existence.

Anatole fouillait à présent avec vivacité dans le coffre.

— Prudence Anatoly ! N'oublie pas que cela fait plus de cent cinquante ans qu'elles t'attendent sans bouger.

La réalité rattrapait Anatole. Une multitude de questions foisonnaient dans son esprit.

— Je vous écoute : inutile que je vous interroge ? Vous me devez bien plus que de simples explications, ne pensez-vous pas ?

La voix de la Comtesse prit un ton protecteur :

— Anatoly, mon Anatoly… J'aimerais tellement te serrer dans mes bras et partager tout mon bonheur avec toi en ce moment précis ! Je t'appelle « Anatoly » pour une raison très claire : tu me rappelles tant mon fils cadet qui lui aussi se prénommait Anatole.

— J'entends bien, interrompit Anatole, mais je ne suis pas le seul au monde à porter ce prénom ! Anatole, Anatoly : quel rapport avec votre fils ?

— Patience et écoute ! reprit la Comtesse. Ne comprends-tu pas déjà ? Tu ne vois pas ? Je t'explique : mon fils Anatoly avait rencontré Frédéric. Presque du même âge, ils s'étaient liés d'une forte amitié.

— Vous voulez dire Frédéric Chopin ?

— Le seul et unique Fryderyk Franciszek Szopen, en effet ! As-tu remarqué mon imitation d'accent polonais ? Je me débrouille bien, n'est-ce pas ? Ah, quel compositeur et quel génie ! Enfin ce n'est pas à toi que je vais apprendre tout cela. Ne t'es-tu jamais demandé pourquoi tu vouais une telle passion à ses œuvres ?

— Non ? Non mais…

La comtesse coupa Anatole sans son élan.

— Ce que tu as entre les mains vaut plus que tout or à mes yeux et, j'en suis certaine, aux tiens également. Te rends-tu compte ? Son art, sa grandeur, sa virtuosité vont finalement renaître entre tes mains ! Peu de temps avant son décès dans notre ville, il avait confié à Anatoly toutes les dernières partitions de ses symphonies inachevées et autres œuvres. Comme tu le disais, tout le monde les croient détruites, même encore aujourd'hui.

Anatole restait de marbre, serrant contre sa poitrine les précieuses feuilles de musique.

— Lorsque je me suis retrouvée ici à mon tour, Anatoly a fait courir cette fameuse légende concernant mon caveau dans l'espoir d'attirer un jour l'unique personne qui devait découvrir ces œuvres attendant leur fin. Frédéric les lui avait données peu de temps avant sa mort comme je te le disais et Anatoly a eu l'excellente idée de les dissimuler ici, au cimetière du Père-Lachaise, avec moi, afin que je veille sur elles. Quand je t'ai vu devant la tombe de Chopin tout à l'heure, j'ai vite compris que nous y étions enfin ! Et que la magie de Frédéric allait vivre de nouveau.

Un long silence s'installait. Puis la Comtesse allait achever son discours.

— Dis quelque chose mon garçon !

— Je… Je ne sais pas, je ne sais plus ! Tout est si confus et à la fois si évident dans ma tête… dit finalement Anatole. C'est comme si tout autour de moi s'était écroulé en une fraction de seconde et que tout s'était reconstruit aussi vite d'une manière féérique… J'ai un profond sentiment de fierté naissante, de responsabilité, de spiritualité : tout me semble normal et pourtant toujours si incroyable !

— C'est normal mon enfant, c'est normal ! ajouta la Comtesse d'une voix caressante. Allons, prends les partitions et referme le coffre. Il est temps pour toi de partir et de te mettre au travail avec toutes ces belles notes qui t'attendent ! Je suis sûre que tu es impatient de les découvrir sur ton piano : tu verras, les dernières mazurkas sont tout naturellement exceptionnelles.

Anatole suivit instinctivement les directives de la Comtesse. Il referma la porte du caveau derrière lui.

— Garde la clef mon Anatoly, garde-la en souvenir de notre rencontre et des liens profonds qui nous unissent maintenant et pour l'éternité.

Anatole glissa la clef dans sa poche, referma la sacoche contenant les partitions qu'il venait de trouver et marcha paisiblement vers la sortie du cimetière.

— Passe lui rendre hommage une nouvelle fois mon enfant quand tu auras déchiffré ses notes : tu lui dois bien ça ! Frédéric et toi étiez de si bons amis…

Le vent de mai soufflait dans ses cheveux. Anatole regarda le ciel parisien dans son crépuscule. Il escalada le petit muret, sauta par-dessus la porte métallique de la rue du Repos et descendit le pas léger sur le boulevard de Ménilmontant. La Ville Lumière ne lui était jamais apparue aussi belle.

About the Authors

MICHAEL ATTARD, *"Oh Canada"*

Michael Attard grew up in the suburbs of Toronto, Canada, and later attended the University of Toronto, where he pursued a degree in engineering. He decided to follow his childhood interest in astronomy thereafter, and completed a PhD in the field in 2009. He has lived and worked in a variety of cities and countries on both sides of the Atlantic, and enjoys a life aimed at gaining as many experiences as possible. Michael currently lives in the Netherlands.

AUDREY M. CHAPUIS, *"The French Table, a Test of Mettle"*

Audrey M. Chapuis, a native of Austin, Texas, worked as a librarian in Chicago before moving to Paris with her husband in 2014. She writes about travel, library lore, women's health and art at AudreyMaryChapuis.com. She also posts daily short-form poems inspired by her new city at HaikuParis.com and is working on a memoir about amateur art appreciation. When she's not writing or botching French vowels, Audrey can be found walking fast, sketching and getting lost in museums. While she couldn't be happier living in Paris, she does miss a good burrito.

ADRIA J. CIMINO, *"Love Unlocked," "In the Red" and "Petit Rat"*

Adria J. Cimino is the author of novels *Paris, Rue des Martyrs* and *Close to Destiny* and is co-founder of indie publishing house Velvet Morning Press. Prior to jumping into the publishing world full time, she spent more than a decade as a journalist at news organizations including The AP and Bloomberg News. In addition to writing fiction and discovering new authors, Adria writes about her real-life adventures at AdriaInParis.blogspot.com. You can learn more about Adria and her work at AJCimino.com or on Twitter @Adria_in_Paris.

SARAH DEL RIO, *"This One Time in Paris"*

Sarah del Rio is a comedy writer whose award-winning humor blog Established1975.com brings snark, levity and perspective to the ladies of Generation X. Despite being a corporate refugee with absolutely no formal training in English, journalism, or writing of any kind, Sarah somehow manages to find work as a freelance writer and editor. She contributes regularly to BLUNTmoms, has made several appearances on the Huffington Post Best Parenting Tweets of the Week List, and her blog won Funniest Blog in The Indie Chicks 2014 Badass Blog Awards. She has also been featured on Scary Mommy, In the Powder Room, and the Erma Bombeck Writers' Workshop.

DRYCHICK, "*La Vie de Vin*"

DryChick is a francophile who spent many a day drinking wine in Paris. She became sober or "dry" not long after she moved to London and was struck by how every invitation revolved around drinking. The message was, if you're not drinking, you're not having a good time. She knew other teetotalers who would rather stay home than face the barrage of questions about why they're not drinking. So DryChick created DryScene.com to get non-drinkers off the couch and back on the town. She writes about her often hilarious experiences being sober in social situations in the hopes that it helps people have a healthier attitude about drinking—just like the French used to have.

LESLIE FLOYD, "*La Dame de la Nuit*"

Leslie Floyd lived in Paris while attending culinary school at *L'Ecole Supérieure de Cuisine Française*. She was born and raised in Austin, Texas and is an active member of the Writers' League of Texas. Leslie has studied extensively under best-selling author Carol Dawson and Texas Monthly Senior Editor Michael Hall. She does calculus for fun, crossword puzzles in ink and fantasizes about a career on Broadway despite a profound lack of talent. Leslie currently cooks, writes and plans future travels in Dallas, Texas with her one-eyed pug, General Cooper, and his sidekick, Sir Ponceycat. Find recipes, reviews and thoughts on the writing life at LeslieFloyd.com.

JENNIE GOUTET, "Driving Me Crazy"

Jennie Goutet is the author of memoir *A Lady in France*, and blogs at ALadyInFrance.com. She also wrote and illustrated the children's book *Happy People Everywhere*, and is a contributing author to *Sunshine After the Storm*, a survival guide for the grieving mom. Jennie was a BlogHer Voice of the Year pick in 2011 and 2013, and her writing has appeared on the Huffington Post, Queen Latifah's website, BlogHer and Mamalode, among other places. She lives just outside of Paris with her husband and three children.

AMY LYNNE HAYES, "(Mis)Adventures at Sacré-Coeur"

Amy Lynne Hayes is a writer and designer based in South Florida. Since her days catwalking the Parisian streets, she has lived in Melbourne, Australia and had a brief stint in Auckland, New Zealand. Her expat days may be over (for the time being) but her love for travel, and all things French, remains strong. Paris is in her blood, and it holds on as tight as the French bureaucracy holds on to its passion for paperwork. Give it time, and you might just spot her sipping wine at a café in her old stomping grounds in Le Marais, an expat once again. You just never know.

APRIL LILY HEISE, "The Glove"

April Lily Heise, a Canadian based in Paris, is an expert on romance in the City of Amour. When she's not getting into romantic mischief, she writes on dating, travel and culture for international and local publications including Frommer's, the Huffington Post, Conde Nast Traveler, City Secrets and DK Eyewitness Guides. She is the author of *Je T'Aime, Me Neither*, a lively novelized memoir on her romantic misadventures and continues to share dating tips, commentaries, true stories and travel features at JeTaimeMeNeither.com.

VICKI LESAGE, "Signs, Signs, Everywhere Signs," "Garden of Eden," and "French Office Workers vs. Zombies"

Amazon best-selling author Vicki Lesage proves daily that raising two French kids isn't as easy as the hype lets on. In her three minutes of spare time per week, she writes, sips bubbly, and prepares for the impending zombie apocalypse. She lives in Paris with her French husband, rambunctious son, and charming daughter, all of whom mercifully don't laugh when she says "au revoir." She penned two books, *Confessions of a Paris Party Girl* and *Confessions of a Paris Potty Trainer*, in between diaper changes and wine refills. She writes about the ups and downs of life in the City of Light at VickiLesage.com. She is also co-founder of indie publishing house Velvet Morning Press.

ELLE MARIE, "10 Things I Learned When My Daughter Moved to Paris"

Elle Marie's books are diverse but all have one thing in common—they reflect her passions. From maintaining a healthy lifestyle (*Living the Thin Life*) to unearthing mysteries (*Chronicle of the Mound Builders*) to visiting her daughter in Paris (this anthology), she writes what she knows and loves. She's never far from her computer; by day she works in the IT field, by night she writes her latest inspiration. When she does step away from the screen, she enjoys spending time with her husband in their hometown of St. Louis.

CHERYL MCALISTER, "A Scoop of Henry"

Cheryl McAlister is an emerging writer, shifting her creative energies from the visual arts (B.F.A. RISD, M.F.A Vermont College of Fine Arts) to fiber art (spinning and knitting with wool from her own sheep) to the literary arena. Her short story "Bit by Bit" appeared in the November 2014 issue of Black Denim Lit. She lived in Normandy from 1984-1985 and has been a dedicated francophile ever since, visiting France as often as possible. Although cutting back on their self-sufficient farming endeavor to give more time for creative pursuits, Cheryl and her husband, Rick, still produce much of their own meat, garden products, canned goods, cheese and hard cider. You can visit her website at NeweStartFarm.com.

EMILY MONACO, "Peut-être"

Emily Monaco is a native New Yorker based in Paris since 2007. She loves caffeinated nighttime wanders, places bathed in layers of history and nineteenth-century French novelists. Emily is the author of TomatoKumato.com, a blog about food, Paris and culture shock. You can also find her at EmilyMMonaco.com and on Twitter @emiglia.

LUCIA PAUL, "Chaperon et Liberté"

Lucia Paul's first trip to Paris was at the age of eight with her family. A love of travel, croissants and window-shopping was born. Her writing includes an award-winning sitcom script, and humorous essays for the Erma Bombeck Writers' Workshop, More Magazine, and Midlife Boulevard. Her stories and essays have been published in multiple anthologies including *Motherhood May Cause Drowsiness: Funny Stories by Sleepy Moms*, *Not Your Mother's Book… On Being a Mom* and *Not Your Mother's Book… On Home Improvement*. She writes about the humor and joy to be found in family and everyday life at DysfunctionalScrapbooking.blogspot.com and on Twitter @DFscrapbook.

DIDIER QUÉMENER, "Half Past Midnight" ("Minuit et demi") and "Le Chemin du Dragon"

Executive chef, private chef, food & wine consultant… Lived in the US, based in Paris: does not wear a beret but eats freshly baked bread every day. Cooked his first meal at age seven, graduated from the Sorbonne, worked as a photographer and finally came back to the kitchen where it all started. Didier is French & American, therefore obnoxious, a wine snob and speaks loudly! When Didier is not cooking, he's writing. When he's not writing, he's playing golf. When he is not playing golf, he's dreaming of being an orchestra conductor, or a guitar player, or… Back to reality: A husband, a father and a foodie! You can find him at DistinctiveParis.com, ChefQParis.com and FoodMe.fr or on Twitter @ChefQParis and @FoodMeParis.

LAURA SCHALK, "The Little Book of Funerals"

Laura Schalk is a lifelong bookworm and lover of words. She's American, closing in on a decade working and living in Paris after stints in Hong Kong, London and New York. She works in the corporate sector and pursues her love of creative writing sporadically, during intensive workshops in the summer and in stolen moments throughout the year. This is her first published piece in a very long time.

BROOKE TAKHAR, "All the Wheat"

Brooke Takhar is a Vancouver-based mama to one goon and busy body to all. She loves the Internet, glittery nail polish, over-sharing and teaching her kid outdated dance moves. She blogs as MissTeenUSSR.com and is a regular contributor to BLUNTmoms.

MARIE VAREILLE, "La Vie en Rose"

Marie Vareille is a French chick-lit author. Her first novel, *Ma vie, mon ex et autres calamités*, a lighthearted story of a young Parisian who flees unemployment and her awful ex-boyfriend by flying away to the Maldives, was published by City Editions in 2014 and will be on the big screen in 2016, via Kobayashi Prod. After living in Paris for years, Marie moved to Bordeaux and works as community and content manager for start-ups. She continues to write fiction on the side, as she has wanted to be a writer since the day she learned to read. She also blogs at Fan-de-Chick-Lit.com. You can follow her at MarieVareille.com, on Facebook (vareille.marie) and on Twitter @Marie_Vareille.

FRÉDÉRIQUE VEYSSET, "Violette"

Frédérique Veysset, a native Parisian, has co-authored three fashion books: *Paris Street Style: A Guide to Effortless Chic*, *You're So French Men!* and *Paris Street Style Shoes!* and is the author of *Daho dans tous ses états*, a book about musician Etienne Daho. As a photographer, her subjects have included actresses Isabelle Adjani and Vanessa Paradis, and her work has appeared in Vanity Fair and Allure. Learn more about Frédérique at Frederique-Veysset.com.

LISA WEBB, "The Best Thing About Living in Paris"

Five years ago, Lisa Webb and her husband swapped their home in Canada for an apartment in Paris. Now living in the south of France with their two baguette-eating daughters, life has become beautiful chaos. When her family isn't in the land of wine and cheese, they can be found exploring the globe with way too much luggage. Lisa writes about her adventures at CanadianExpatMom.com, and on Huffington Post, BLUNTmoms and Parentdish.

ANNA WEEKS, "An Attempt to Explain the Paris Fandom"

Anna is an aimless wanderer, currently meditating on what's next for her. She is an avid reader who sometimes writes sarcastic reviews of erotic short stories for various bloggers around the interwebs. Due to a silver-lined layoff from her corporate job, Anna recently moved to Omaha, Nebraska with her rowdy cat in order to pursue her creative interests. With the help of her best friend, she created, produces and stars in the Type Omaha podcast, which explores the cultural oddity that is the city of Omaha. You can follow her on Twitter @anna_saurus_rex and follow her podcast @TypeOmaha.

APRIL WEEKS, "Whine Country"

April is an attorney, cheese-monger and blogger extraordinaire. She currently lives in Atlanta with a 4-year-old monster, two matching Siamese cats and her ever-patient and understanding husband. When she's not reading or chasing ambulances she... well, reads some more. She's the sole curator of TheSteadfastReader.com. She desperately misses living in Europe and is willing to negotiate her immortal soul for a legal job in London. Since she's a reader, not a writer, she has published nothing else of interest, unless you're interested in papers on American tax law.

DAVID WHITEHOUSE, "*Les Urgences*"

David Whitehouse finds non-fiction easier and less revealing than fiction. He has written a book on the question of Rwandan genocide suspects in France, *In Search of Rwanda's Génocidaires: French Justice and the Lost Decades*. He was the ghostwriter for the autobiography of long-time Cambodia opposition leader Sam Rainsy, *We Didn't Start the Fire: My Struggle for Democracy in Cambodia*.

Acknowledgements

First and foremost, Velvet Morning Press would like to thank author Stephen Clarke for setting our Parisian stage by writing a foreword for this anthology. *Merci* for capturing the multi-dimensional spirit of Paris, Stephen!

A big thank you to all of the writers who shared their work in *That's Paris*, as well as those who submitted pieces for consideration. Thank you for writing about this amazing city! We are glad Paris offered you inspiration, and we hope the City of Light will continue to illuminate your beautiful creative minds.

Thank you to Ellen Meyer for making the anthology look lovely, and *merci* to Gisèle Quémener for assisting with the editing.

A thank you to the book bloggers who have agreed to read this anthology and write about it on their blogs. As publishers and authors, we appreciate all that you do to support our industry!

We also would like to extend a *grand merci* to Valérie Ferrière of the U.S. Embassy in Paris for supporting Velvet Morning Press and our authors.

And finally, thank you, readers and Paris-lovers. We hope this anthology has transported you to the beauty and diversity of Paris.

About Velvet Morning Press

Velvet Morning Press is a boutique publishing house that discovers new authors and launches their careers. VMP publishes fiction in a variety of categories, short story anthologies and special projects.

Adria J. Cimino and Vicki Lesage are the women behind VMP. Both authors themselves, Vicki and Adria use their experience in writing, editing and marketing to bring the work of other writers to bookshelves. VMP's anthologies include *Legacy*, *That's Paris* and *Christmas, Actually*.

If you enjoyed this journey to Paris, please consider leaving a review on Amazon—even just a few sentences!

Want more? Get *Recipes and Reads* for free! Simply join Velvet Morning Press's new release mailing list: http://bit.ly/vmp-news.

A taste of the good life in...
Recipes and Reads

You know that feeling you get after you turn the last page of a great book? It's similar to the feeling you get after enjoying a delicious meal. Satiated. Pleased. Relaxed. Yet... eager for the next slice of goodness!

So, as publishers, readers and food-lovers, we decided to pair our favorite indulgences into this appetizing guide of great reads and great recipes.

Get it for free! Join the Velvet Morning Press new release mailing list and we'll send you a free ecopy of *Recipes and Reads*: http://bit.ly/vmp-news.

If you like *That's Paris* you might also like:

29846489R00166

Made in the USA
San Bernardino, CA
31 January 2016